A Song of Strength

To my little ones

Never let the future overwhelm you

Your passion will help you suceed

Prologue

The tranquility of the gardens always calmed Femi, helping her concentrate whenever she had a problem. Bees buzzed around her, the occasional bejeweled hummingbird darting by her head in search of nectar, as she hummed to herself. Small tendrils of gold sprouted from the earth, twisting its way in intricate little curls until a collection of small golden flowers came into bloom. Eyes closed, Femi basked in the sunlight that fell on her face, her raven locks framing her face and drifting down her back in thick waves.

Delicate pink blossom petals swirled around her as they dropped to the earth, their fragrant aroma lending to the serenity the shamasal was feeling. Her whole world turned upside down earlier that morning when she'd felt her gift receding as she attempted to stop the bleeding of a young woman suffering from a difficult child birth. By the grace of the gods, both the mother and the baby survived, but it would be a long road for the mother's recovery.

The gentle splashing as a turtle slipped into the little pond in the corner of the garden while a light breeze rustled the water lilies helped with her meditation. As the ripples spread to the outer perimeter of the pond, Femi used their soft waves as a way to amplify her thoughts. With each ripple, she recalled a specific moment during the birth where she felt her powers slip. Songweaving did not falter. This meant one thing: Femi's time as the shamasal of Shuu was ending and it was time for the new shamasal to assume their position as songweaver.

A soft noise pulled Femi from her thoughts. Eyes still closed, she pushed through the fog and left her meditative state. Whoever stood off to the side cleared their throat once more, not wanting to interrupt the shaman, but still demanding her attention nonetheless.

"To what do I owe this pleasure, Honorable Father?" Femi's voice came out in a husky purr as she mentally said a prayer of thanks to the gods for the knowledge they imparted upon her during the reflection. "Casual visitors are so rare."

"I heard about the young woman," Asim replied. His words, though blunt, were not accusatory. Instead, they were laden with concern. "Femi," the shaman turned to her leader. "These are uncertain times. My father never worried about having to send someone to N'aanzthal as an offering to the gods. I don't want this blood on my hands."

Femi's heart sank. If she wanted to prevent unnecessary deaths, she would need to find a replacement and train them in the art of songweaving, and fast.

"Finding my successor and training them may take a while," she replied, her voice hesitant as she tried to ignore the ramifications. "Perhaps we should choose our first sacrifice now and conduct the ceremony from the shadows. There is no need to worry Shuu."

The High Chief took a moment to absorb everything, giving Femi a reprieve so she could say a prayer to the gods asking for guidance. She had no clue where to start looking for the new shamasal. When Parvenah, her master, had approached her, Femi remembered how baffled she'd been. Asking the woman how she knew Femi was the right choice led to more questions.

"It's a feeling of rightness," Parvenah had said. *"Just like when you're healing through songweaving, just as you know what you need do to mend bone and flesh, the same applied when I found you. I looked at you, and felt your... essence. It's hard to explain, but you'll know when the time comes."*

"Femi," Asim finally said. "Do your best to find your successor. Pray to the gods that we aren't making the wrong decision. I'll consult the bones to see who our sacrifice is. By their will, we will only have to perform the ceremony once."

A darkness blanketed the High Chief's visage as he voiced his decision. Femi couldn't blame him, the New Moon Ceremony required them to offer the heart of the chosen one to the gods. Their blood was to be mixed with a sacramental wine before being thrown into the holy fire in Khons' temple to protect Shuu for another year. She would never want to make that choice either.

And yet, she had to. The fate of Shuu rested on her ability to find and train the next shamasal before the new year, Tepet. The prospect daunted Femi.

▼△▼

Being out in Shuu when it wasn't Tepet felt unnatural. After living in her room up in the mountains for ten years, Femi forgot what it was like to walk among her people, like a regular person. A simple white dress with embroidered flowers on the collar and her thick hair done up in a braided updo, Femi found herself wanting to avoid the stares of her people. Of course, she couldn't ignore the reverence showered on her by the countless people who walked up to her and pressed their foreheads to the back of her hand, murmuring words of gratitude and adoration in hopes of receiving a divine blessing from the holy woman.

Every time, she obliged. Femi learned long ago to push away her discomfort for the sake of her people. And every time, they would walk away beaming, feeling reassured with whatever problems they had in their lives. At least their smiles made it worth it as they scuttled away.

Faces came and went, all a blur, as she casually made her way through the streets. Femi often found herself humming in an effort to calm herself, small flowers popping up in her wake much to the delight of those sharing the road with her. Nothing resonated with her, drawing her towards any one person.

Laughter caught Femi's attention. Just ahead, a family with three children rounded the corner. The eldest snacked on sweet breads, while the two youngest skipped beside them, happily enjoying the snack as well. The parents meandered behind their children arm-in-arm, lost in conversation. As she gazed upon the family, Femi felt a familiar tingle course through her body. It was exactly as Parvenah had said.

The shamasal found herself humming as she studied the five, a trio of golden butterflies materializing unconsciously. She stopped when the young girl gawped at the butterflies before running over. The girl's eyes sparkled as she babbled away about the magic unaware of who Femi was at first. Her elder brother pulled her back, apologizing to Femi for his little sister's indiscretion while the youngest brother clamored for more butterflies.

Femi laughed, the innocence of the girl, not even old enough to be considered a young woman, refreshed the shamasal. A feeling of serenity washed over her, while at the same time, the tingle became stronger, sending shivers all over and causing goose flesh to prickle on her arms. Staring into the young girl's eyes, Femi felt a pang of regret. She'd found her successor in this ten-year-old girl.

I

CHIONE STOOD at the altar, dagger in hand. The stifling smell of incense hung heavy around her. Gripping the dagger in her sweaty hand, Chione sighed. She hated this part of her duties. Why couldn't the gods have given shamasal a better way to enhance their powers?

"Songweaving is not all child birth and bringing our stories to life," Femi would always say. *"It's healing the sick and mending wounds too."*

At the top of the altar sat a small stone bowl filled with water from the sacred pool behind the temple. Stepping up to the bowl, Chione raised her arm over it. She closed her eyes and took a deep breath as she moved the dagger across the back of her forearm, creating a shallow cut. Her breath caught in her throat as the sharp pain seared the back of her arm.

Bright red droplets of blood dripped down her arm and stained the dagger. She placed the blade down on the altar and dipped two of her fingers into the holy water. Raising the wet digits to face level, Chione drew an intricate figure in the air — a rune of power.

Then, she stepped away from the altar and returned to her pillow. Kneeling on the temple floor next to her master, Chione began singing. Her voice was pure as she coaxed the healing energies within her to bind up the wound, just as Femi had taught her.

Deep vocal tones resonated against the stone walls. Faint gold lines began to form around her whole arm. Moving to her middle range tones, Chione sought to focus her power. The gold lines moved down to her forearm, encircling the cut. As the wound began to glow with a gold light, Chione switched her singing to high-pitched barks, entreating her ancestors to help her finish. Like sinew cords, the golden lines crossed the cut multiple times, as though it was sewing the skin back together.

A warmth flowed where the wound used to be, and a thin gold line marked where the cut had previously been.

"Very good, Chione," Femi said. Her master's warm voice was filled with pride at the feat. "Soon we will be able to expand your training to healing others."

Making her way to the altar, Femi offered a prayer of thanks before picking up the dagger and wiping it on a piece of cloth she brought with her.

Chione got up and joined her mentor at the altar. "Do you think I will be ready to lead soon, Femi?"

Trepidation filled the young girl as she imagined herself taking the mantle from Femi and being responsible for the people of Shuu. Four years of training did not seem like enough time for their lives to be placed into her hands.

Femi looked at Chione, a smile playing on her lips. "My dear, no one truly knows when they will be ready for the gods' call. All you can do is learn as much as you can and hope that when the time has come, you will have learned enough from me."

"But the elders are pushing for me to finish my training."

Femi tutted and dipped her fingers into the bowl. She sprinkled some of the holy water onto the blood-stained cloth, mumbling a prayer before stuffing the rag into her waistband. "We do not work on the elders' schedule, my child. You will know once you are ready to take over."

Placing the dagger back on the altar, Femi beckoned Chione to follow her out of the temple into the bustling streets of Shuu.

"Come, Chione, Tepet has begun. I must head out and attend the ceremonies. Join me."

A thrill coursed through Chione at the news. It had been much too long since she'd been able to participate in the New Year celebrations. Just the thought of enjoying all the sweets available made her mouth water in anticipation.

Throngs of people wove through the roads, heading towards the center of the city, a drastic change from the path down from their mountain temple. Women carried woven reed baskets with them as they headed to the marketplace, their white dresses contrasting against their dark skin. Their hair hung down loosely on their backs, accented occasionally with a brightly colored feather. Those with straight hair had a few smaller braids along the side, while others let their curly hair bounce freely.

The women chatted merrily amongst themselves while their young children raced in between them chasing each other. Chickens clucked in the streets, dodging the travelling populace. Men strolled at a leisurely pace, joking with their friends. Their long hair tied back in a tight, high tail.

Chione took in the riot of colors that surrounded her. After spending her early teenage years training with Femi in the temple dressed in the same cream-colored gown day after day, she missed having the opportunity to wear her gold jewelry or her linen wraps that accented her white cotton dresses. Despite the heat of a normal day in Shuu, the outfits were quite breathable. On those rare occasions, Chione would have worn her chest wrap and skirt. Looking at what she could no longer wear, Chione felt a small pang of regret as she contemplated her future as a holy woman.

She smiled as she watched her eight-year-old brother, Nkosi, running through the streets with his friends. The boys ran both bare-chested and barefooted on the hot stones. As they rounded a corner, Chione caught Nkosi's eye and she waved slightly. Nkosi smiled and waved back, before following after his friends.

"He's getting so big," Femi mused, her eyes glowing.

"I know," Chione murmured as she recalled her isolation in the temple focusing on her studies. "I can't believe it's been four years already. I wonder how Mother and Father are doing."

A pang of regret brought a tear to her eye as she thought of all the time she'd lost up in the mountains. By order of the High Chief, Chione had been sequestered away in hopes of expediting her training. Four years of missed Tepets, yearly birth celebrations, and warm hugs from her mother filled her with a wave of emotion.

"I'm sure that we'll see them in the square. I've heard that your older brother has been selling his carvings at the weekly markets. Rehema showed me one of them, and I must say that they are very good."

"Really? I'm surprised that Meskhet found time to devote to something other than tchlatsi," Chione giggled. "He always wanted to challenge our warriors to a game when we were growing up."

"Ahhh, tchlatsi," Femi said with a smile. "I haven't watched a game since I was a girl. Perhaps we can take the whole day off and enjoy the festivities as long as we make sure to return to the temple at dusk to do our evening prayers. Tepet will not be ruined if we indulge a little."

"Are you serious?" Chione asked, hope blooming in her chest. Could they really take the day off from training?

Pausing, Femi tapped her forefinger against her lips. "What would the consequences be for relaxing during our new year festival?" she hummed.

A moan of longing escaped Chione's lips, causing her to blush as soon as she realized that she made an audible sound.

Finally, Femi broke the tension. "I think we've earned a nice break. My master, Parvenah, was more traditional and would not allow for me to take a break from my holy duties. I must say, it made me quite tired after all those years. I don't want you to grow weary of your sacred duties, my dear. The gods created these holy days so that all may celebrate, us included."

Chione lost all of her decorum for a brief moment as she began spinning around in the streets, throwing her arms up in the air in excitement. After three rotations, she composed herself and looked properly ashamed at her actions. As a shamasal in training, Chione wanted to not bring disgrace to her family by losing herself in childish pleasures.

Femi laughed, a deep, earthy sound. As she laughed, several thin threads of gold swirled around her body. A golden butterfly, more shadow than substance, flitted about through the shimmering threads. Several people stopped walking and stared at the rare display of magic, most having never seen their shaman at work. A few children started chasing the butterfly image, their hands grasping at the ethereal creature.

Femi stopped laughing as those around her greeted her by gently grasping her hand and bringing it to their forehead. Each time a person paid respect to her, Femi would quietly inquire about the health of a loved one or offer a blessing. Several of the people walked over to Chione and did the same thing once they finished with Femi.

Chione stood awkwardly, unsure of what to do, when a number of elderly women took her hand and brought it to their heads. A couple of the women even kissed her hand after bringing it to their forehead several times. After being sequestered from the people from several years, she never experienced a Tepet as a shaman. All of the rituals and duties that were expected of her seemed so strange. Even the warm sunlight on her skin felt surreal having only enjoyed the sun from the gardens since the mountain temple usually lay hidden in the shadows of the trees.

"Blessings from Mother Muut, may you feel her bounty," was all Chione could say. All of her teachings went out of her head at the shock of being one worthy of the greeting.

After the last of the citizens paid their respect to the two women, Femi placed her hand on Chione's shoulder in much like her mother would have done.

"Now that you're in your fourth year of training, people will expect more from you, Chione," she said. "The eye of Khons now focuses on you. As surely as he will give you guidance, our people look to you to share that wisdom. Make sure that you stay calm and remember the holy principles. They will never fail you."

"Easy for you to say," Chione mumbled. All of the attention discomfited her. "You have lifetime of experience, and I have almost none."

"Chione, I've served our people for twenty-five Tepets," Femi said, her expression determined. "The eye of Khons has almost completely left me. You must be ready for when my time passes and yours fully begins."

Chione was taken aback at the unusually harsh demeanor of her normally cheerful master. All she could do was nod silently in hopes of not offending Femi. Time seemed to move slowly as she waited for Femi to say or do something, although only a few seconds actually passed.

Finally, Femi beckoned Chione forward with her towards the center of the marketplace. Chione followed wordlessly as the two continued on. As they neared the heart of the city, Chione took in all of the beauty of Shuu on Tepet.

The outsides of homes and businesses were scrubbed clean and fresh, and white dahlias were placed around the doorways in hopes the gods would bless them with good fortune in the new year. Linen clothes of deep blue adorned the sides of the shops, hoping to entice the gods into bringing them good luck and prosperity in the upcoming year. Golden figures accented with turquoise stones were displayed in the windows of the white mud houses, each one depicting one of the gods or the great panther that saved Shuu from the Darkness.

Chione marveled at a gold figure of Maah-res, the great panther. Her lithe form could be distinguished even in the precious metal. Two emerald stones were placed in its head where her eyes would be. In the morning light, the emeralds sparkled with a fire, making Maah-res look alive. The big cat's mouth was opened slightly, exposing her deadly fangs. Besides Maah-res lay a smooth black stone with a poem of protection written on it with yellow ochre.

"Mother Muut wrap us in your arms," Chione whispered as she read the poem.

"Come, Chione!" Femi called out.

Breaking her gaze from the statute of Maah-res, Chione realized Femi had moved on without her. She stood several yards away, smiling at her. Chione jogged over to her master, weaving around the moving masses.

Femi stood a few paces away from a small, wooden makeshift stand. Attending to a young couple, Chione let out a gasp of surprise as she recognized her older brother, Meskhet. As soon as the couple left his stall, Meskhet turned and spotted his sister. Butterflies filled Chione as she saw her brother's eyes sparkle in delight as he noticed her standing just a few paces away.

"Chione," he said beaming. "I'm surprised to see you out of the temple." Spotting Femi, he bowed his head in deference to the revered healer. "To what do I owe the honor of your presence, blessed Femi?"

"The pleasure is mine, my son. I've just brought young Chione out with me to enjoy the festivities since she has been doing so well in her studies. A reward, you could say."

"I'm pleased to know that my sister is doing well. She has brought much honor to our family with her being chosen to carry on the will of the gods."

"She has indeed," Femi said with a smile. "Now, if you'll excuse me. I've just spotted some sweet breads that I simply must have. Meet me by the flower girl's stall so that we can plan our afternoon meal. You'll need to eat soon to help you recover from this morning's activities."

"I'll make sure to eat something before we meet up again," Chione replied.

With a wave of the hand, Femi turned and began making her way to the pastry stand. Chione and her brother watched the shaman saunter off before returning back to each other.

Chione stared at her brother once more. He'd changed so much, just like Nkosi. Instead of the lanky youth that she remembered, he'd put on a little weight and gained muscle. His previously long hair was now kept short. Surprisingly, it made him look younger than when he kept his hair longer. As she gazed at her brother, Chione felt distinctly aware that of her body as she stood awkwardly in front of him.

"You've grown," Meskhet said with a smile. "The aunties have been talking about you lately. They seem to think that since you haven't become a full shaman, you still have time to look for a husband."

Chione turned a deep shade of red. "Meskhet, you should be the one looking for a wife. You're four years older than me and should be working to carry on the family name."

Meskhet held up his hand and gestured to the carvings in his booth. Wooden figurines of Maah-res, a hawk that represented Khons, a nude woman to represent Muut, the giant turtle Shetwea, and several other great beasts that terrorized the ancients of Shuu. There were carvings of all sizes, but the majority were only a couple inches tall. The rich grain of the wood was dark and smooth, showing off the minute details that her brother added.

Hidden in the corner of his wooden booth, Chione noticed a few loose precious stones, several lengths of deep purple and crimson linens, sweets, and a leather pouch that was filled with coin. There did not appear to be a large store of wood carvings to replace what he sold.

"Meskhet is doing well for himself," Chione mused.

As she watched her brother turn his attentions to another customer, Chione noticed a young woman walk over to the booth. She leaned casually on the side of the booth and watched him market his wares. The girl was lovely, with a curvaceous frame and long legs. Flowing locks of thick, wavy hair cascaded down her shoulders and rested gently on the middle of her back. A hibiscus was nestled in her hair behind her right ear, and a delicate golden chain hung around her neck.

Meskhet pointed to a medium-sized carving of Shetwea to his customer. The statue's shell was carved from a lighter colored wood than the body. The man looked at Meskhet's suggestion and commented on its beauty. Her brother glanced towards Chione and noticed the young woman leaning against his stall. A smile played at his lips as he continued on with his customer. His admirer smiled back and waited for him to finish with his business.

The man made an offer to Meskhet, hoping to save a few coins by offering to have his wife to weave a blanket in exchange for the statue of the holy god. Meskhet looked over at the woman leaning against his stall near Chione once again before nodding his head in approval. The two men shook hands as Meskhet handed over the carving. As soon as he sold the figurine, Meskhet turned to the girl and beckoned her into his booth.

"Ashatiqa, I told you I'd meet you when the sun is at its highest," Meskhet said.

"Sharrat and Enanatuma are too busy trying to find boys to buy them something to eat," Ashatiqa replied, her voice deep and husky. "They think that by rubbing against some guys the right way, they'll get free food." Ashatiqa rubbed Meskhet's hand and arm as she spoke, flashing an alluring smile.

Chione stared at the young woman in disbelief. Meskhet caught her reaction and laughed.

"I'll meet up with everyone once I clear up here. I'll close up shortly," Meskhet told Ashatiqa.

Ashatiqa walked off with a slight pout on her lips. Her eyes, however, failed to mask her amusement.

Once Ashatiqa was out of sight, Meskhet turned back to his little sister. "I met Ashatiqa last Tepet," he explained. "Don't tell Mom and Dad, but I'm saving my money to ask her parents to unite with her. I've almost got enough, I think." He beamed as he spoke about his plans.

"Oh, Meskhet, I'm so happy for you!" Chione gushed. Her older brother finally getting married would be a gift to their family. Chione wondered if she should hug her brother, or stay where she was. Choosing to remain where she was, Chione asked, "Will you have the unity ceremony in the temple? I would love to bless your union. Have you spoken to her about your plans or will you surprise her?"

"I wanted to surprise her."

Before Chione could say anything else, an older woman stepped up to his stall and started admiring the remaining wooden figurines. As soon as she started to ask questions about the product, Chione caught her brother's eye and motioned that she was going to leave.

"NaeNae, let's try and meet up later to talk," Meskhet said.

"I would like that," Chione replied. Waving good-bye, she left her brother's booth and made her way through the marketplace.

II

CHIONE PASSED a number of wooden stalls as she headed towards the center of the city. Stands selling produce lined the streets, interspersed with ones selling cakes, kebabs and other goods. The scent of coriander, anise and cardamom filled her nostrils, making her mouth water slightly. Memories of Tepets from her childhood eating kebabs and sweets with her brothers brought a smile to her lips. One in particular stuck out. She was only six, but Chione vividly remembered the vibrant colors of the setting sun as she and Meskhet huddled together eating some honey cakes. A thin golden chain rested on her wrist, a gift from her parents to celebrate her moving from the youngest child to the middle. Behind Chione and her brother, their parents held the two as they watched the sunset, Chione's mother's round belly pushing against Chione's back. As the sun went down, marking the end of the old year and start of the new, Chione felt the baby kick.

Pulling herself from the memory, Chione eyed the savory snacks with a longing, but knew that she should not grab a bite to eat until she'd seen all of the booths. One booth carried a variety of sun cakes that she used to love when she was younger. Making a mental note of the booth, Chione continued on, but promised herself that she would pick up one of the tasty morsels before the festival was over.

A few trinket booths caught her eye as well. Men and women selling jewelry, finely dyed linens, and statues carved out of turquoise or bronze. Chione stopped at several of the sculpture vendors to check out their work. As a child, she'd always begged her parents for one of the beautiful items, only to be told that she wasn't yet old enough.

She spied a beautiful turquoise figure of Shetwea at one of the tables. His eyes were flawless onyx stones that were polished until they reflected the image of whoever stared within. His shell contained veins of gold leafing that crossed through. The effigy's opulence overshadowed the carvings of the other gods and goddesses. Statues of Niu-met, Kekhtet, Atarghaat, Khons, Maarduk and Muut, all delicately carved out of turquoise, lay scattered on the top of the stall.

Something pulled her attention from Shetwea's piece to the Sisters. Kekhtet's flowing hair cascaded down her slender frame, enclosing her perky bosom. She sat perched atop a polished carnelian stone. The eldest of the Sisters, Kekhtet, was the epitome of beauty and the envy of the other goddesses. Her sister, Atarghaat, sat gracefully atop a jasper stone. Atarghaat was a mermaid, her coy smile barely concealing her fanged teeth. The goddesses of darkness and death respectively, their eyes, even in the lifeless stones, looked a bit sinister.

Next to the sisters stood Niu-met, the mighty jackal who ruled over the void that greeted those who sinned in life. His glass orange eyes shone against the turquoise color of his canine body. Form tense and ready to pounce, Niu-met's half snarl made Chione's stomach drop.

Skimming over the forms of Khons, Maarduk and Muut, Chione found her eyes being drawn back to Shetwea's carving. Dragging her fingers against the mighty god, she lightly brushed against his head and shell. With a flash, Chione saw a startling scene in her mind.

A young boy lay on the smoothed stones, a gaping hole in his chest leaking blood down his torso and onto the ground beneath him. His eyes were still moist, tears running down his terrified face. Darkened figures in background wailed in despair as High Chief Asim walked back to the holy sanctuary with the bloody dagger. Chanting from the people of Shuu drowned out the cries of the boy's family, calling out to the gods and begging for their protection in the upcoming year.

Chione's stomach dropped again as she watched the horror unfold. In a panic, she tore her gaze away from the lifeless body and slowly followed the retreating form of Asim. Off to the side, a stone dais bearing the young boy's heart served as the center of the ceremony. Chione tried to ignore the grotesque sight and looked into the throng of people.

At the back of the group, a shadowed figure stared back at her. Its dark eyes stared at her with an intensity that turned her disgust into discomfort.

Shaking her head, Chione took her fingers off of the carving and looked around at the other tables. Apart from the turquoise Shetwea, she did not see any other works that were of the same quality as her brother's. Rushing away from the statue of Shetwea, Chione looked for Femi amongst the crowd. Her world spun as she tried to process what she'd just seen as her heart pounded in her chest.

Was that my first vision? Chione wondered, bewildered. *Am I just tired from my earlier training?*

Chione staggered through the throng of people milling around as they waited to the afternoon's festivities to commence. The bodies appeared distorted, the effects of her vision still plaguing her mind. With each step, her heart calmed and her vision cleared, pushing Chione's panic down once more.

A deep rumbling in her stomach startled Chione, causing her to make a quick detour at a kebab stand and grab a small bite to eat. Snatching a morsel of spiced lamb from the spit, Chione chewed greedily. The juices dribbled down the side of her mouth as she took another bite from the kebab, taking a piece of onion with the lamb. She wiped her mouth with the back of her hand absentmindedly as she looked for her mentor. With each bite, a little more clarity filled her with serenity.

Femi's head bobbed into sight next to a cake stand. She spoke animatedly with another woman in between bites of a sweetened treat. Chione quickly finished her snack and placed the greasy stick in one of the wooden waste boxes and hurried over to her instructor. As she neared Femi, she thought the other woman looked familiar. Accompanied by nearby warriors, the woman stood off to the side of the main crowd. She wore a great egret plume in her wavy, dark hair. Thick gold bangles covered her arms and dangled off of her neck. Small turquoise stones dotted the chunks of gold in her necklace. As Chione neared, she recognized the woman Femi was speaking to as Eshe, wife of the high chief. Having only seen her once before at the temple, Chione wondered what the two could be speaking about.

"Ah, Chione!" Femi called out with a smile. "Did you have a nice time with your brother? I was just talking to our Honorable Mother about your progress."

"Sister Femi believes that you may be ready to move onto healing others," Eshe said. "Do you think you are up to the challenge in the event that we have an injury during our tchlatsi match later today?"

"I — oh yes, Honorable Mother," Chione stammered. "It would be an honor to heal one of our great warriors." Chione ducked her head slightly and dropped her eyes, unsure if she should be showing more deference to the leader of her people or if she was allowed to face her directly.

Eshe chuckled and said, "Sister Chione, it would be our honor to be able to help you achieve your great potential. Shetwea knows we need you to complete your training as soon as possible. We won't have Sister Femi with us forever."

Chione felt her stomach knot. Femi had told her before that the time would come, but Chione still didn't feel ready. What if Femi lost her gift before Chione felt comfortable with her control over her powers? She knew she wasn't nearly as strong as Femi.

"Oh, don't you worry, Honorable Mother," Femi said. "Chione will be ready before you know it."

"I'm pleased to hear that," Eshe replied. She looked at the two shamasal and nodded to them before bidding them farewell. Her guards followed her a short distance behind.

Once Eshe was gone, Chione turned to Femi in shock. "Femi, how could you promise her that I'll be ready to take over for you soon? I have so much more to learn. I can't possibly be ready by when Great Eshe would want. I don't even think I can heal the tchlatsi players in front of everyone."

Cupping Chione's right cheek in her hand, Femi slowly moved it down to Chione's chin. Her expression was soft as spoke to the young girl. "My dear, you don't even understand how little you have left to learn. You are so close to completing your training, soon you won't need me."

Chione stood silently as she absorbed her mentor's words. Her chest filled with pride as the knot in her stomach loosened, a feeling that she hadn't experienced since she was chosen by the gods to be Femi's successor. She couldn't believe that Femi had so much faith in her when she felt so inadequate.

"I'll do my best to make you proud," Chione whispered.

But I'll never compare to you, Chione thought. *No one else has been chosen by the gods for such a long time as shamasal. You perfected songweaving.*

"I already am," Femi replied.

The sound of singing permeated the general chatter and noise of the busy market. A light aria from one of Shuu's altos announced that the high chief had a proclamation to make. As one, everyone in the market square made their way to the stone dais near the temple of the gods, Baah-re.

"I wonder who will be playing in the tchlatsi game today?" Chione asked. "I heard that Po'tchai will be participating this year."

As one of Shuu's elite warriors, Po'tchai was a favored tchlatsi player by the populace, especially the women. A game played with a leather ball and stone hoops from which the teams can score if they knock the ball through, the players wore no more than a cloth covering to ensure their modesty, leaving their impressive physiques on full display. Po'tchai in particular, drew large crowds whenever he was allowed to play. Chione remembered her mother being especially fond of the man whenever he walked onto the tchlatsi field, his muscled figure standing out as sweat gleamed on his flesh. Chione felt herself flush as she thought of his impressive body.

"Po'tchai? I would be surprised if Honorable Father allowed for someone of his caliber to risk injury in tchlatsi."

"That's a good point."

"Unless," Femi said with a mischievous grin, "this is what our Honorable Mother was talking about."

Chione's jaw dropped as she stared at her master, wide-eyed. "No," she whispered.

Femi laughed. "I'm sure that they would not do anything that would put Po'tchai in any form of danger. You probably just heard some juicy gossip."

"You can't tease me like that!" Chione cried, flailing her arms as she walked. She then blushed furiously as she realized that she was walking through a heavy crowd of people, several of whom actually turned to look at her as she flapped around like a chicken. Chione dropped her eyes in embarrassment as her face remained flushed.

"I'm sorry, Chione," Femi said, barely suppressing a laugh. "I should be more dignified for one of my position." She then burst out laughing, the musical sound causing a riot of golden flowers to pop up on the side of the street, catching the eye of a number of people in the moving crowd.

Many people came over to the two and offered themselves in respect to the two shamasal. Sucking in a deep breath and being rewarded with the mouthwatering aromas of the nearby stands' delicious temptations, Chione pushed away the butterflies in her stomach. Holding onto the scents as long as possible, Chione found her embarrassment subsiding and she allowed the crowd to take her hand in theirs as they pressed it against their foreheads. The two women smiled at each person in response as they walked away after paying their respects to the two shamasal.

Once the last person left the pair, Femi turned to Chione and smiled. "Well done."

The aria was getting louder as the crowd approached the dais. At the head, the imposing figure of High Chief Asim stood waiting for the last stragglers to arrive. Standing shirtless in his ivory wrap, his strong form demanded respect. At his side were his wife on his left and the young woman summoning the populace, a temple maiden in a cream dress, on his right. Behind the leader, the warriors of Shuu stood at attention, dressed in simple loincloths.

Chione and Femi settled towards the back of the crowd. Chione looked around and spotted her parents standing to the side with Nkosi. With a start, she saw her friend's Yahya and Shani milling around by her family. Shani's head turned a bit and she caught Chione's eye. Elbowing Yahya, the two waved at their friend. Chione waved back enthusiastically. Excitement filled the young shamasal as the two turned back to face the

Honorable Father. She hadn't seen the two in almost four years, ever since she was first brought to the temple to begin her training, and seeing how much they'd changed made her both happy, but left her feeling a little sad that she'd missed out on experiencing everything with them.

The crowd became quiet, causing Chione's head to snap back to the dais. Asim stood in front of the dais, arms outstretched.

"Children of Shuu, Great Khons smiles upon us today and has blessed us with beautiful weather for our Tepet." Asim's strong voice carried all the way to the back of the crowd. "Before we move forward with our festivities, it is my unfortunate duty to choose our next chosen one to travel to N'aanzthal."

A heaviness filled the air at this announcement. Up until now, the atmosphere had been cheerful. Chione swallowed, trying to push down a lump that appeared in her throat.

Is this the duty that Femi mentioned? she wondered as pockets of murmuring broke out amongst the crowd.

Raising his hands to silence his people, Asim waited until he had their full attention before speaking once more. "I know this is difficult for all of us. I do not enjoy being in this position, but we must make sure that the gods are placated for another year. Until our new shaman has completed her training, we must continue this practice."

"Honorable Father!" a voice called out. It belonged to an elderly woman with milky eyes. Her long hair was tied in a braid that she'd thrown over left shoulder. "We've already sent four people to N'aanzthal. Surely last year's sacrifice was more than enough."

Sacrifice? Was *this* the holy offering ceremony?

Asim's eyes looked pained, while Eshe's head drooped.

"Who was last years?" Chione whispered to Femi as voices around her murmured in agreement to the elderly woman.

"Thoeris entered N'aanzthal at the will of the bones," Femi said softly, her voice catching in her throat.

Chione sucked in her breath loudly at the news. The Honorable Mother's own mother and a beacon of light, Thoeris had acted as a grandmother for all of the children of Shuu, telling them stories of the olden days and singing songs in her slightly cracking, but heady voice. How could the gods demand such a person be sacrificed?

"She entered N'aanzthal with quiet dignity," Femi continued. "When she walked into Baah-re, the mourning ceremony lasted a full moon cycle before Honorable Father asked that we move forward with our lives once more."

"Is that why you send me into the caves for meditation for so long every Tepet?" Chione asked.

Femi nodded.

Chione's eyes dropped as the people around her pleaded for mercy, insisting that Thoeris' sacrifice should hold more value than the rest of Shuu. As silence replaced the protestations, the heaviness returned once more. Chione rubbed her arm, uncomfortable knowing that she was the reason that four, soon five, people were killed in order to appease the gods. Tears dripped down as she blinked rapidly, cursing herself for being so slow in mastering her teachings.

Why did Femi not push me to learn faster? Why did no one tell me of this?

It took the chief a long while before he could speak again. "N'aanzthal is not a merciful place. Everyone is equal in her realm. Venerable Thoeris is no more valuable a soul than anyone else." Asim's face was pained as he paused. "My children, it is time to see whom the bones have chosen."

As one, the people of Shuu collectively held their breath. Chione was surprised to see Femi making her way towards the chief carrying a golden platter laden with chicken bones.

When did she leave me? She was just right next to me. Chione's head whipped around, surprised that anyone could move through the packed crowd.

Femi kneeled down and placed the platter on the ground. She rose slowly and backed up as Asim reached down and collected the bones into his hands. Femi stood by the dais as Asim shook the bones between his cupped hands.

One.

Two.

Three shakes and he dropped the bones. They landed together with a clatter that was amplified by the tense silence.

Asim looked at the bones for a long time, sharing a glance with Femi, before speaking. "It has been decided. From our Great Mother's side, it will be the third child of our third family."

A woman began wailing. Several more joined in as people began figuring out the family line.

"Third family..." Chione muttered. Her brain worked to figure out who was the third line from the Great Father and Great Mother.

The keening turned into screaming.

Chione turned towards the source of the noise and watched as Yahya's mother clutched her youngest son, Tarik. Yahya buried her face in her hands as her father tried to comfort her mother. The people standing around them backed away, leaving Yahya and her family grieving together in an open circle.

"Father!" Nena cried. "He's just a boy! Take me and leave my son!"

Asim shook his head slowly, unable to look at the grieving woman.

Nena shrieked and collapsed onto the ground, wrapping her arms around Tarik's legs. Tarik stood in shock, tears streaming down his face as he worked to understand what had just happened. Yahya grabbed him into a hug, only to be pulled into his father's embrace along with their other son. Held tightly by his family, Tarik sobbed quietly into her shoulder, his tiny arms clutching at his sister.

Chione looked around and watched as Nkosi began to cry. Her mother, Naeemah, rubbed her son's cheek, wiping away his tears. Several other women continued to wail as they shared in Nena's pain. Eshe wiped her eyes with her hand as she stood by the dais. Femi gathered the bones and placed them back onto the golden platter before hurrying away.

Asim raised his hands once more, silencing all but the grieving family who stood, still isolated, from the throng. "Subira family, you are welcome to join the chosen in Baah-re and partake in his feast. Your son will eat a meal fit for the gods before he joins them in N'aanzthal."

Two of the warriors made their way to Yahya and her family, escorting them away from the main group. One of the warriors picked up the sobbing Nena and carried her in his arms as they headed into the holy temple.

Once the family disappeared inside the sanctuary and the wailing faded away, Asim addressed his people again. "Now, it is time to celebrate our Tepet with our traditional tchlatsi game. I know that it can't overshadow the darkness that is to come later today, but I hope that we can find some measure of light in the festivities of this holy day. Let us move towards the field."

Waving his hands once more, Asim dismissed his people and began to make his way towards the tchlatsi pitch. Eshe and the warriors followed suit. Slowly, the crowd broke apart, following the Honorable Father to the playing field.

Chione watched as her family was one of the last to leave. They stared at Baah-re, their eyes glistening and pained. Femi walked over to her pupil and pulled Chione into a hug.

"I'm so sorry that you had to see this," Femi whispered into her ear. "This is why I haven't let you go to Tepet. I didn't want you to see the consequences of the gods taking my gift or burden you further with the duties of being a shamasal."

A wave of emotion flooded over Chione and she burst into tears. Femi tried to comfort Chione by making shushing noises before starting to hum softly. A solitary flower bud to materialized at Femi's songweaving. As Chione cried, a golden butterfly appeared, struggling to fly. Resting on Femi's flower, it flapped its wings, but couldn't get enough strength to lift off.

Femi's humming got stronger, causing the bud to open up, revealing a beautiful blue lily. Chione took several shuddering breaths, working to steady her breathing and stop crying. Her butterfly began flapping its wings a little faster and the movements became stronger. After a couple attempts, the butterfly managed to lift off of the flower and fly away. As it flew away, it dissipated into nothingness. Taking her cue from Chione's relaxed breathing, Femi stopped humming and her flower disappeared.

"Come, Chione," Femi said. "Let's go back to She-weh."

The young girl rubbed her eyes and nodded. Taking the lead, Chione walked back to the temple, Femi following behind her. The pair wove through the throng of people. Some talking animatedly about the upcoming tchlatsi game, having pushed the bone ceremony to the back of their minds since their families were not affected by the gods' decision. Others moved somberly, the weight of the proclamation still heavy on their souls.

"The bone ceremony was created when there was a shift in power between shamasal," Femi explained. "Normally, it's done when the acting shamasal dies, but once I felt my power begin to disappear, the Honorable Father had to consult the bones after the gods came to me during a long period of meditation. Their sacrifice protects Shuu while she is most vulnerable."

Their journey to the playing field seemed to drag on for an eternity. Chione watched as the older generation shuffled along, talking softly amongst themselves. Femi walked by her side, listening to their conversation.

"It's a shame about the Subira family," one silver-haired woman said to the other. "Their boy was so sweet."

"He's too young," a younger woman said. Her hair was long and dark, but had a grey streak going through it. "I wish we had an age limit. Where do we draw the line?"

"We should've drawn the line at Thoeris," the first one said. "She was a once in a lifetime woman."

The other women in the group all nodded and murmured their agreement.

"It's a shame we can't just ask the gods to give us time since they got such a great soul last year," the grey-streaked woman said. "Imagine if they let us postpone the sacrifice because we have a shaman-in-training. Surely, she's almost done four years later."

The herd of women diverged from the two shamasal when they took a different street. The duo found themselves walking down a relatively deserted road towards She-weh.

"Have you ever wondered what it would be like if we could speak with the gods?" Chione asked Femi. "Wouldn't it be great if we could change such ancient practices? It's not like they do much for us nowadays."

"You speak of dangerous things," Femi replied. "To speak so casually of our protectors, you are showing quite a bit of disrespect."

Chione dropped her head, eyes staring at the smoothed stones that made up the street.

"On the other hand," Femi said with a smile, "wouldn't it be great to change the old ways and save future lives?"

Chione's head snapped up and she stared at her mentor. "Do you think it could work?" she asked excitedly.

"We won't know until we try." Femi pat Chione on the back, drawing a smile from her. "While I finish some tasks that need to be finished before Tepet's end, go to your room and try to contact the gods. We don't have much time if we want to save the boy's life."

The two entered the temple, acknowledging the greetings from the bowing temple maidens, with a sense of urgency. Femi nodded to the women and headed out to the back room while Chione rushed to the altar. Panic welled in her breast as she lit the incense and dipped her finger into the basin of cool water next to the door before drawing a rune of clarity and guidance. With forceful concentration, Chione struggled to keep her breathing steady even as her chest continued to tighten. Rubbing her hands together, Chione noticed that a thin layer of sweat slicked her palms as her hands trembled.

"Oh, gods," she muttered to herself. "I can't do this."

With a deep breath, Chione closed her eyes, counted to ten, and opened herself to the gods, praying they would be receptive to her call as she walked through the altar room door.

III

FEMI WALKED into her room and sat down on the edge of her bed. Pulling over a silver basin filled with water, she dipped a cloth into the cool liquid and began cleansing her feet. Jasmine petals floated in the water, releasing their refreshing aromatic scent into the room. The water soothed her aching feet, eliciting a soft moan as she massaged the bottom of her foot with the rag.

Once she finished wiping down her feet, Femi walked to the woven basket in the corner of her room and picked out a small bottle of rose oil. She pulled the top off of the glass carafe and dabbed a bit of the oil on her forehead between the eyes and on each side of her neck, right under the jaw. Replacing the lid on the bottle and returning it to the basket, Femi then closed her eyes and drew a rune of wisdom into the air in front of her.

Rubbing her hands together, she grabbed a piece of sandalwood incense, using the flame in the small stone pit in the corner of her room that warmed her room to light the incense. Femi placed the incense on the floor and sat down on the red mat at the foot of her bed. She closed her eyes once more and drew a rune of guidance into the air. She wondered if she would get a response from the gods. As Chione's training progressed, Femi found it harder and harder to communicate with the gods. In the altar room, Femi knew Chione was fervently trying to reach them to save her friend's brother. Inexperienced, Chione very well could encounter one of the less understanding gods and potentially anger them. No, Femi knew that she must reach out to the gods as well. It might be her last chance to help her people.

Femi began to hum, and tendrils of gold grew out of her body in soft wisps. They curled around her, pulsating in rhythm with her humming. A flood of colors entered her mind. Femi worked to find a cohesive image amongst the explosion of colors. She sat on the ground, focusing on her breathing until the incense burned out, but nothing came to her.

With a sigh, Femi got up and stretched her legs. She then bent down and wiped up the remains of the sandalwood, tossing them out of her room's window. Disappointed, Femi sat down on her bed.

"Why could I not see anything?" she murmured as she rubbed her eyes. "Are the gods blocking me?"

A gentle breeze blew through her window, carrying the scent of rose with it.

"There's no roses around She-weh," Femi murmured.

The smell grew stronger as she tried to decipher the meaning behind the roses. Returning to her mat, Femi drew a rune of clarity before closing her eyes once more.

▼△▼

Chione entered the main altar of She-weh. Walking up to the water bowl, she anointed herself with the holy liquid. Then, she walked to a silver basin to purify herself. As she washed her dusty feet, Chione forced herself to focus on her breathing in hopes of stopping her hands from shaking. Inhaling and exhaling slowly, she worked to clear her mind as she breathed. After countless attempts at contacting the gods over the years, Chione silently prayed that someone would answer her call. Femi's instructions played over in her mind, reminding her to still her heart and mind if she wanted the gods to speak to her. Her breath came out ragged as she hoped one of the Sisters did not respond; she knew she wasn't ready to bargain with the likes of them. After finally managing to calm herself, Chione looked for the sacred oil to anoint herself with, along with the incense to light. Once everything was prepared, Chione sat down at the base of the altar and closed her eyes. Drawing a rune of wisdom, Chione exhaled as she opened herself to the gods.

A world of color greeted her as she meditated. Streaks of white sped towards her while splashes of various hues raced in the background. Suddenly, everything went black. Chione looked around and found herself alone in the darkness. Only a faint light could be seen glowing in the distance. Standing up, Chione took a few tentative steps. Her footsteps echoed loudly in the emptiness. Squinting her eyes, she tried to find what she was supposed to be looking at.

After several long moments, she turned behind her. She heard water dripping in the distance. Her chest tightened as her breathing sped up. Nothing like this had ever happened to Chione before. Remembering Femi's words to remain calm, she calmed her fear. There was much at stake and she couldn't wait any longer.

"Seems like the best way to go," Chione said softly.

Despite whispering, her voice echoed, leading her to believe that the place was larger and more cavernous than she believed. Her heart began racing as her excitement at entering the holy realm set in.

Chione wandered aimlessly in the near darkness. Occasionally, a brilliant streak would fly overhead, startling her. Her feet sounded like thunderclaps, and she could've sworn that she could hear her heartbeat pulsating around her. Time felt like it stopped while she walked. All Chione could do was try to focus on the rhythmic beating of her heart to help her gauge time.

After what felt like an eternity, the flashes of light were consistently golden in color. They also zoomed overhead more frequently. Chione noticed that her footsteps no longer echoed like they once did, but she thought she heard her heartbeat change rhythm. The sound was more complex, and the beat was faster than it had previously been. Chione started to worry as she brought her fingers to her neck, feeling her pulse, as she worked to slow her breathing.

"Steady," she murmured.

The rhythmic beating got louder as she continued forward. With her fingers to her throat, she realized, that it wasn't her heart beating in some strange pattern, but a separate heart beating in rhythm with hers. Panic began to set in as her mind filled with thoughts of her spirit being destroyed by angry gods.

If anything happened to her mind in this realm, what would happen to her physical self? The countless possibilities put her on edge and she found herself wiping her sweaty palms on her dress several times.

"What's in here?"

Almost in answer to her question, the second beat got louder. It thumped in a frenetic off-beat pattern that mesmerized the young shaman. Chione moved slower, unsure of whether or not she should get closer to the sound. The beating got to be so loud that she had to cover her ears with her hands. Chione froze in place as she struggled to focus her thoughts over the cacophony that surrounded her. The rhythm filled her every pore, threatened to engulf her entire being and make it its own. Chione tried to push the invading noise out of her, but it was strong. Too strong.

In an act of desperation, she let out one pure note of panic. The sound filled her and pushed the thumping out of her body. Her body relaxed as she gained control once more. Just as quickly as the beats became unbearable, they stopped altogether. Silence filled the darkness. Chione breathed a sigh of relief and took her hands off of her ears.

Suddenly, a multitude of golden flashes pierced the darkness streaking across the sky. One after the other, the lights sped overhead before crashing into the ground mere yards from where she stood. The ground shook with each smash, bringing Chione to her knees. She whimpered as she tried to steady herself enough to get up and run.

After what felt like ages, the streaks finally stopped and silence returned once more. Chione managed to stagger to her feet, wiping away a few tears from her eyes. None of this was what Femi had prepared her for. Looking around, she saw darkness once more. The young shaman had enough and wanted out of her vision and decided to make a run back to where she started.

Why do you run after summoning me?

Chione froze in her tracks.

"Summon?" Chione managed to squeak out. "I... I don't know. This has never happened before." Her answer was rushed as she spun her head side-to-side, trying to find the source of the voice.

Do you know who you've awakened?

The voice filled the space she stood in, penetrating every fiber of her being, yet somehow, not deafening like the heartbeat.

"Please, if I could know who I am speaking to," Chione pleaded, "I could properly address you."

She struggled to maintain her composure. Her mind raced to the few gods she did not want to meet. Maarduk, the cunning fighter, and the Sisters of death and darkness were high on that list. Known for their volatile tempers and disagreeable personalities, they'd be less likely to listen to her pleas.

The voice chuckled.

Very well.

A brilliant white light filled the blackness, blinding Chione. She brought her hands up to shield her eyes. After the initial burst, she lowered her hands, and Chione could make out a silhouette approaching her, but she couldn't see any details. Her eyes ached as her pupils dilated. Finally, the brightness died down, and all that remained was a faint glow illuminating the shadowy figure who stood before her.

Chione squinted. The person before her was tall and lithe, and they had long hair. Their body was humanoid in shape, removing Shetwea, Maah-res, and the Sisters as a possibility. She breathed a small sigh of relief and tried to focus her eyes on the details of the figure.

As more of the being came into view, she recognized the body to be a male body.

"Not Mother Muut, or Kekhtet," she murmured. Much to her pleasure, her voice didn't echo like it previously had.

Examining his face, Chione tried to discern who it was. The face resembled that of a cat. His eyes were yellow, and the pupils were black slits. Though he didn't have any whiskers, Chione could imagine one of the strays that frequented her temple and recognize the similarities.

Dropping to her knees and placing her head on the floor in front of her, Chione said, "Greetings, Blessed Khons. Your appearance is a blessing upon me."

Khons smiled at the young girl, causing Chione to gasp. Unlike his more feline features, his mouth was wide with thin, razor-sharp teeth instead of the expected canines like a cat. His ears twitched as he watched her with amusement.

Why have you come to N'aanzthal? Khons asked.

His voice rang in Chione's head. She opened her mouth to respond but closed it in confusion. Why didn't she hear an echo? Surely there should be one. Raising her head, she stared at him, trying to keep her fear under control.

"I... -I come to seek an audience with the mighty ones," she began. "I am Oduolam Chione, daughter of Khafra. My master is Haz'dellah Femi, holy shaman of Shuu. I ask that you hear my plea to grant us a safe and prosperous year, but still sparing the life of Subira Tarik," Chione continued, heart racing and cheeks heating up. "He's just a boy! My little brother's the same age as him. He still has so much life left to live, and it's not fair that he is to be the sacrifice just because I haven't completed my training yet."

Khons stood, face impassive, staring straight at Chione. His ears wiggled occasionally, but his eyes showed no emotion.

Chione's heart dropped into her stomach as she realized that she may have offended the god. And Khons was not just any god. He was the younger son of Mother Muut. Though he was known to be more even-tempered compared to his older brother, Maarduk, he was still a high god in the pantheon.

"I'm so sorry," Chione said, head on the ground once more. "Please forgive my insolence. I spoke out of passion. I meant no disrespect, Blessed Khons."

Rise, my child, his voice commanded.

Almost against her own will, Chione found herself taking her head off the floor before she could even process what he said. The young shaman sat on her knees, hands resting lightly atop her thighs, waiting for his next command.

You come for noble reasons, seeking a respite for your people. Do you know why the sacrifice is needed?

Chione shook her head.

Khons motioned for her to get up. Again, her body reacted before her mind had a chance to respond. She found herself on her feet and approaching the god within seconds. Once she was in front of him, Khons placed his hand on her forehead.

Instantly, Chione's mind flashed to a processional moving down the streets of Shuu. The houses lay strewn on the dirt streets, much sparser on the land than what Chione knew. She looked around and found that she barely recognized anything. The communal garden was a dirt patch with rocks scattered throughout, and the statue of High Chief Elulu wasn't in the town square. The statue was erected before her parents' parents were born. Chione wondered how long ago her vision occurred.

White flowers covered the dusty streets. Chione wandered along, passing the slow-moving people, to see who the ceremony was for. She was surprised to find that she ended up at She-weh. In front of the stone dais, High Chief Elulu stood somberly. Next to him lay the body of a young man, not much older than Chione. The man was surrounded by the flowers, and the line of mourners did not appear to end, flowers in hand.

The ground rumbled, eliciting screams of fright from the people. Some of the stones from She-weh cracked, rubble falling to the floor. Elulu jumped to the side, narrowly avoiding being hit with some of the debris. Flowers that surrounded the deceased spread out along the ground.

Once he gained his footing, Elulu shouted for calm. "Brothers, sisters, we must not fall to the terror that we've been facing. Though we have lost Brother Arwium, the gods have not forsaken us. The fact that we are still here for the ground tremors proves that we can see the next day."

"High Chief, is it true that Maah-res stirs? Is she the cause of our shudders?" The voice came from an elderly woman who had already placed her flower.

As more people shuffled forward and placed their flowers, Chione noticed that the end of the line neared. The people at the back of the procession looked nervous, glancing around as they stood close to their neighbor. She then turned to look at their chief. His face showed his uncertainty.

"My sister," Elulu said, his voice carrying through the city and reaching those at the end of the line. "Do not fear the panther. I have an idea that may appease the gods. It is, a rather unpleasant one." His eyes dropped as he spoke. "If we sacrifice one of our own, perhaps we can stave off their wrath until we find a new shaman."

An uncomfortable hush fell over the crowd. The last of the mourners dropped their flowers off at the body before quietly blending in with the rest. Not so much as a peep could be heard. Feet shifted in the dirt, creating a few small puffs of dust amongst the group.

"I know that I cannot ask this of you, so I will offer myself to them. Please be kind to my son. Treat him with the same respect that you did to me."

Elulu's eyes misted over as he glanced over at his wife. Chione noticed that the chief's eyes lingered on the young woman's stomach.

"She's with child," Chione murmured.

She watched as the woman began silently crying. Her hand gently squeezed her son's shoulders. Turning to his mother, the boy buried his head in her dress and wept.

"Blessed Elulu," the older woman from before spoke, "are you sure that it is wise? Where would we be for guidance during your absence?"

"My sister, I cannot ask something of you that I would not be willing to do myself. Trust in the gods. With my death, it is my hope that they will protect you all and guide you to a new shaman."

The next day, Elulu sacrificed himself on the altar at the Temple of She-weh, Khons said. ***My mother and I were so moved by his selfless gesture that we went down and found a way to quiet the earth. Before the year was over, Mother Muut chose a replacement, a young woman named Sabit, and the practice was put to rest. It wasn't until shortly before Haz'dellah Femi's time that another sacrifice was needed again.***

Mother gets busy, Khons continued, ***and sometimes forgets to choose a successor for Shuu. When you were chosen four years ago, I don't think she realized that your age would make the transition take longer than usual. Ten is much too young...***

Chione looked up at the slender god. His eyes lingered on the high chief as he walked over to his wife and ran his hand through her hair. Her eyes were warm. Reaching up, Chione found that she had started to tear up. The scene faded away, and Chione found herself standing in the darkness once more.

"What can I do to make sure this doesn't happen again?" she asked. "No one should have to experience this type of pain."

Khons was silent for a long time. A soft hum emanated from him. Overhead, several brightly colored streaks soared across the heavens, their length and brilliance changing with the pitch of his voice.

My people have come to expect an offering to ensure Shuu's protection, he said slowly. ***It is because of this that Kekhtet and her sister do not seek more from my brother. I don't think I can convince them to accept otherwise.***

His voice was heavy. Chione wasn't sure, but it almost seemed as though the god actually sympathized with her plight.

"But what if there was another way?" she asked.

Such as?

"Perhaps each province could sacrifice a yak or goat in their holy temple. We have shrines to each god throughout Shuu. By offering the prized beast, possibly even yearly, we can sate the goddess' desire for flesh and spare our people."

Chione hoped her suggestion would at least intrigue the gentle god. As Khons pondered the effectiveness of such an action, the humming returned once more. This time, the sound was louder. The flashes returned, moving faster than they had previously. They were accompanied by golden sparks that showered down into the emptiness. Chione held her breath, praying that she'd done enough.

Finally, after what felt like an eternity, Khons spoke.

My child, I believe that may work.

Chione's chest filled with hope and a smile broke out on her face.

"Oh, Holy Khons, I am so honored that —"

I did not say that it would, Khons interjected.

Chione's face fell as the short-lived hope quickly faded.

But it is our best option. Return to your body. I must speak with my mother. I will let you know her decision before Tepet has ended. Change is not accepted in N'aanzthal so easily. Hopefully she will be receptive to your plea.

"Thank you, Holy Khons," Chione said.

A white light engulfed the two, blinding Chione. Squinting her eyes open, Chione looked around and realized that she was back in her room. Birds chirped in the distance. Her incense lay burned to ashes on her bedroom floor. Getting up slowly, Chione almost fell to her knees. Her legs were asleep.

A soft knock on her door forced her to push herself upright.

"Enter."

Femi walked into the room. Her eyes were puffy, as though she had not slept for days. All of the excitement and questions Chione had regarding her vision with Khons disappeared as she rushed over to her master and guided the woman to her bed.

"I just had the most incredible experience!" Seeing the woman's distress, Chione rushed over, reaching out tenderly for Femi's hand. "Did you see something? What happened?"

"What did you say to them?" Femi questioned, her tone sharp.

"I... I... uh asked them to reconsider the sacrifice," Chione started, rubbing her hands together as she stared at her mentor. "I asked if maybe we could use something else, like a yak or goat."

"Chione, who did you speak to?"

"I spoke to Blessed Khons. I didn't think he would, but he actually listened to me."

A sudden gust of wind entered Chione's room, bringing with it, rose petals. The candle on her floor flickered violently but did not extinguish. Petals swirled around the two. Once the wind died down, the petals fell to the floor, but the scent of roses lingered in the air. Femi and Chione looked down at the petals.

"My dear, I believe that if we move quickly, we can still catch Asim."

Hope returned to Chione quickly blew out her candle before she and Femi dashed out of the room, leaving the moon-shaped rose petals undisturbed on the smooth stone floor.

IV

"MY CHILDREN!" Asim called out to his people.

As the chief spoke to the crowd, Chione and Femi stood next to the Honorable Mother. Femi, having cleaned herself up after entering Chione's room earlier that morning, held Chione's hand, occasionally giving it a light squeeze. Their meeting with Asim and Eshe after the signs the two shamasal received brought forward fresh hope. Asim had sent a warrior to Baah-re to bring the Subira family back to his home, postponing the sacrifice.

"I ask that everyone treat tonight with the utmost respect," the chief continued. "Our Sisters have spoken with the gods and secured our salvation. In exchange for our souls, the gods have agreed to take a yearly sacrifice of each province's prized yak or goat. Starting today, we will sing praises to the gods as we celebrate until the moon has returned to N'aanzthal. Now, go and complete your offerings. They must be done before the sun has crossed the horizon."

A roar broke out from the crowd as the people of Shuu celebrated. Neighbors hugged and cried, grateful that the human sacrifice had been ended. Nena and her husband hugged Tarik. People kept walking over to them and offering their support and well-wishes to the family. Tears streamed down Nena's face as she thanked everyone.

That night, the people of Shuu feasted in celebration of the new Tepet rituals. Yaks and goats burned on the altars, the fat dripping into the flames, causing them to spark and sizzle. Music and dancing played deep into the evening. In the light of the fire, elders told their families the stories of the gods, re-enacting the great battle between the brothers, Maarduk and Khons, over the land.

By the time that the first rays of the sun stretched into the sky, the fires had died out and the people had returned to their homes to sleep. Only the crackling of the dying embers and the grunting or bleating of the animals could be heard.

V

"Maarduk!"

Kekhtet's voice rang through the halls of N'aanzthal's great palace, K'iitzche. The cool marble floor muted her hurried footsteps as her figure quickly appeared. Golden columns and a myriad of brightly colored flowers sparkled in the brilliant sunlight as butterflies flitted from flower to flower, sipping their sweet nectar. The goddess' long gown flowed behind her, her legs flashing through her high slitted dress and ample bosom threatening to spill out with each rushed step.

"Maarduk!" she called once more. "Where are you?"

Stretching languidly, the god looked up from his chaise. Sweeping a curtain of hair out of his black eyes, he replied with a bored drawl: "What is it, Kekhtet?"

The goddess stomped over to the slumbering god, a miasma of blackness forming behind her. In her anger, tendrils of the darkness extended, reaching towards the lithe god.

"It would appear that Man has dishonored us," she growled. Her normally husky voice was laced with anger.

"How so?"

"Their new shaman has not completed training," she spat. "If the Time Weavers are correct, we should have been offered a sacrifice this Tepet in order to ensure our protection."

"I've enjoyed the offering they gave us. In fact, they were most generous this year and provided each of us with one." Maarduk lay back down on the chaise and rolled over.

"They gave us animals, not their finest warriors!" Kekhtet cried. "When Elulu spoke to Father, he promised us that in exchange for our protection, Shuu would give us their finest whenever they were in between soothsayers. Well, Niu-met has told me that they are in need of one. Why do we not have our due?" Kekhtet threw her arms over her head, lifting her gown up perilously high.

"Calm yourself," Maarduk said, pulling himself back up to face the angered goddess. "Let's speak with Niu-met and see what's going on. Man knows of the deal they made long ago. They wouldn't break their word to us so easily. Not when we give them so much."

Rising, Maarduk got out of the chaise and motioned for Kekhtet to follow him. His lithe form slunk ahead of the fuming goddess, his tail swishing back and forth in time with his steps. The god cracked his knuckles and rolled his neck, trying to wake up.

"Maarduk," Kekhtet began.

Snarling, Maarduk turned to face the woman, his dark eyes narrowing at her. "I'm not in the mood for anything more, Kekhtet. Silence."

The goddess kept her mouth shut, only to hiss softly in anger. The two exited the halls and entered the garden. On the edge of the pond, Atarghaat relaxed, combing her seaweed green hair. She glared at Khons, who lounged on a rock. As they passed into the garden, the air rippled around them, stripping them of their magical gifts and dissipating the blackness that surrounded Kekhtet. Maarduk couldn't help it as the corners of his mouth twitched upwards as the enraged goddess let out another hiss.

"Welcome, brother," Khons greeted. "What brings you here to Everpeace?"

Atarghaat hissed at the younger god. She clenched her bone comb, snapping one of the teeth in her hand and piercing her skin. Her sister walked over to her and sat down. Kekhtet dipped her legs into the pond.

Maarduk stared at his brother. Anger slowly bubbled within him. Seeing Khons always seemed to do that to him.

"Well, brother, Kekhtet and I were looking for Niu-met. She seems to think that Shuu has disrespected us."

Khons arched an eyebrow at his brother, his slitted eyes nonplussed.

"They have!" Atarghaat hissed. "Khons over here spoke to Muut — Mother Muut," she said at a glare from both of the brothers, "and convinced her to allow Man to give us a paltry gift in exchange for our protection."

"It's not a 'paltry gift'," Khons replied. "This is a yearly offering to honor us. How could we not accept their prized sacrifices? This way we all get one."

"Brother," Maarduk said. "I can't believe you would talk Mother into this. I'll have to speak with her and correct this."

"It's too late, brother," Khons said with a smile. "Mother has gone and spoken to Shetwea about the matter. He agrees that this is a better alternative and has written it down in the books of the Time Weavers. It is now a binding agreement."

With a roar, Maarduk lunged towards Khons. He crossed the distance to the rock quickly and reached out for his brother. As if he ran into an invisible wall, Maarduk stopped abruptly and was thrown backwards. Atarghaat and Kekhtet screeched as he landed roughly on the lush grass.

"Now, now, Maarduk," Khons taunted with a wicked smile. "You know that there is no violence in Everpeace. This is most unbecoming."

Rubbing his back as he sat up, Maarduk glared daggers at his brother.

"How could you make a decision like that without consulting the rest of us?" he snapped.

"Their shamasal asked nicely," Khons replied simply.

Maarduk got up and started pacing around the perimeter of Everpeace. Low growls rumbled out from him as he fumed. Occasionally, he slashed at a tree, leaving long gouges in their trunk. With each strike, the trees returned to their original, unblemished form. The rivalry between the sons of Mother Muut flared up once more as Maarduk realized that Khons had found a way to undermine the system he'd set up centuries ago. It didn't matter that there would be a yearly offering to the gods. His blood boiled as he looked at his brother's smug face. After several long minutes, Maarduk stopped. Taking a deep breath, he turned to face his brother.

"If it is in the books, then so it shall be. If I were you, brother, I would not venture out of Everpeace anytime soon," Maarduk snarled. "There is only so much the sacred lands can do to protect you. Come, Kekhtet."

Standing, the goddess gave her sister a confused look before following Maarduk out of the protective walls of Everpeace. Atarghaat remained behind, glaring at the lounging Khons. As the duo left the tranquil grounds, their powers and strength returned to them.

"Maarduk, what are you going to do?" Kekhtet asked. Their time in the hallowed garden seemed to have brought a measure of calm to the previously agitated goddess. "We can't go against Father and Mother Muut."

Maarduk ignored the question as he continued forward. Inside he was fuming, but he knew that he must focus on what he needed to do. If he played his hand right, he'd get his true sacrifice and also show his brother why the old ways should not be changed.

The pair hurried through the grounds and out into the forest. Kekhtet looked around uncomfortably, rubbing her arms as they went deeper into the woods, but Maarduk ignored her. He strode ahead, letting his thoughts consume him. As the darkness loomed before them, the trees thinned out until they reached a clearing. At the heart of the clearing, a shaft of light broke through the branches, illuminating the area.

Maarduk stopped abruptly, causing Kekhtet to almost run into him.

"Why did you stop?" she hissed.

Maarduk shushed her and motioned for her to stay behind him. "Keep quiet and let me do the talking," he instructed.

Kekhtet nodded and slunk behind him. There was darkness behind the pale strip of light in the clearing before them. Beyond the light, neither could see anything. There was no sound in the forest either. No chirping of birds or burbling of the stream that ran through the woods not too far from where they stood. There wasn't even the sound of cracking wood on the jungle floor from any deer or other creatures. It was unnerving.

Maarduk drew up the bottom of his shendyt, revealing two golden circles, one on each leg. On his left leg was the symbol of power; his right had the symbol for summoning. Closing his eyes and growling softly, Maarduk gently tapped the runes. At his touch, they began glowing with a bright golden light.

A heaviness fell upon the two gods. Kekhtet looked around, startled, as she nearly dropped to her knees with the force of the weight.

"What are you doing?" she struggled to say.

Maarduk ignored her. His face was set and sweat began beading on his brow. For several long minutes, the force pushed down upon the two. The pair stood silently, straining to hear anything in the desolate woods. The beam of light flickered in the clearing, creating shadows on the forest floor.

A low growl floated through the darkness. The weight lifted and Maarduk heard Kekhtet breathing heavily next to him. Glancing at the goddess, he noticed that perspiration lightly covered her forehead and arms. Maarduk was also covered in sweat, but did not appear to be struggling like the goddess. Kekhtet worked quickly to regain her composure as she noticed his gaze upon her and wiped the sweat off of her body.

Out of the darkness, a large panther gradually emerged from the blackness. Her feet padded mutely on the forest floor as she entered the clearing. The feline's fur, onyx with a hint of a metallic sheen, was a stark contrast against her vibrant yellow eyes.

Her eyes.

That is what drew the attention of both of the gods. Filled with a fierce intelligence, marking her as different from other creatures. Her eyes narrowed as her pupils dilated in the bright clearing. The panther spoke, her voice a deep rumbling growl.

"Why have you summoned me?"

Maarduk bowed, motioning for Kekhtet to follow his lead. The goddess curtseyed, bending her knees slightly and dipping her head, but not breaking eye contact with the massive beast.

"Venerable Maah-res," Maarduk said as he straightened his body once more. "I come asking for your services."

"You confuse me for someone who cares about the politics of N'aanzthal," Maah-res growled. "I've told Muut time and again, I do not want to be bothered. I served my time for her cause back when we fought against the Darkness ages past."

She turned slightly and used her huge paw to part her fur. Underneath lay a jagged scar that covered the majority of her left leg. Her fur returned back to its normal place as she removed her paw. The goddess' tail twitched with her displeasure.

"Your service has not been forgotten, Mighty One," Maarduk quickly said as he dipped his head once more in reverence to the panther, his mother's sister and equal to Shetwea. "However, it appears that Man has forgotten all that you sacrificed for them."

The panther's eyes narrowed.

Taking that as his cue to continue, Maarduk pressed forward. "If they could just be reminded of *your* power. I ask that you go down and show them that they cannot disrespect the gods without consequence. A single reminder is all that I ask."

Maah-res stood silently. In the sliver of light, her coat shone a lovely metallic hue. Her claws protracted and retracted, digging furrows into the ground.

"Please, Mistress," Kekhtet spoke up. Her voice sounded strained, and her eyes were filled with despair. "We only came to you because we knew that you command such respect from all who meet you. We would never dare disturb you otherwise." Her eyes teared up as she spoke. Clutching her partially exposed bosom, Kekhtet's bottom lip trembled.

Maah-res' glanced from Maarduk to Kekhtet several times. Her tail swished as she weighed everything she'd just heard. After a lengthy silence, a bemused smile crossed her feline lips.

"Very well," she said. "You have my service. But only one."

The panther began to purr, a low rumbling from deep within. Her claws flashed in and out of her feet once more.

Dropping to his knees, Maarduk placed his balled fist against his chest. Kekhtet followed close behind, mimicking his actions and dipping her head so that her eyes stared directly at the ground this time.

"You have no idea how much your actions mean to me, Revered Maah-res. Might I ask that the example you make is one of the elders? I feel that would have a more lasting effect that just killing a farmer in the outer districts," Maarduk said.

"I make no promises," Maah-res replied, eyes narrowing slightly. She stopped purring. "Just be glad that I'm going down there at all."

"Understood," he replied.

As silently as she came, Maah-res turned around and disappeared into the darkness once more. All that was left was the sheen of her pelt as it reflected in the thin beam of light. Soon, even that was gone and the two were alone in the clearing once more. All residual heaviness that hung in the air completely disappeared. Birds could be heard chirping and off in the distance the burbling of the stream could be heard splashing off of rocks.

Motioning with his hand, Maarduk instructed Kekhtet to trail him. The two made their way out of the forest in silence, and dense tree growth returned as the pair traveled through the woods. They continued on their way until the scent of moss could be smelled once more.

Once they exited the copse, Maarduk turned to Kekhtet, who took that opportunity to walk by his side.

"You surprised me," Maarduk said, smirking as he glanced at her. "Who would've thought that princess of darkness could cry? You Sisters are supposed to have hearts of stone."

"Oh stop," she gushed, pushing his arm in a playful manner. "You embarrass me."

"I'm serious though. We were about to lose her if you hadn't spoken up."

Flipping her hair, Kekhtet flashed a sharp-toothed grin. "Then you owe me a favor."

Maarduk stopped in his tracks. "Excuse me? I wouldn't have done this if you hadn't come to me."

"You were the one who was angry because of your brother's actions," she reminded him. "I didn't tell you to enlist the help of the great panther."

Kekhtet turned around to gloat when Maarduk's hand shot out and encircled her neck. Her eyes widened in panic as the god gripped tightly. His dark eyes were hard. The goddess struggled to gasp out a cry, but couldn't. Her hands scratched at his, trying to break his grip. Maarduk grabbed the hair on the top of her head and yanked hard, throwing her off balance. The goddess' hands flailed, struggling to remove his iron-tight grip from both her head and her neck.

Maarduk pulled her in close and hissed into her ear, "You play foolish games if you think you can demand a favor from me. If I were you, I would choose my next words carefully."

Kekhtet squeaked out a response, her eyes starting to flutter as her body threatened to pass out.

"Do you understand?" Maarduk asked.

Kekhtet tried to nod. Her knees buckled.

Maarduk released his hold on the goddess, who fell to her knees, gasping for breath. She clutched at her neck and head as she struggled to recover. Her eyes watered as she wheezed.

"Now, what was it you were saying?"

Gasping for breath, the goddess choked out, "I didn't say anything. I'm just pleased that our efforts were rewarded with a positive outcome."

Smiling, Maarduk replied, "As am I."

The god began walking once more. Looking around her, Kekhtet tried desperately to find an excuse to leave. Unable to find anything, she started jogging after Maarduk.

VI

MAAH-RES LET OUT A SIGH as she walked into her cave. She made her way to her favorite rock and began scratching at it, sharpening her claws. If she was going to do a job, even on the mortal realm, she may as well do it right.

Flashes from her battle with the Darkness crossed her mind as she worked. Faceless beings with long fingers ending in claws, known as the Whispers, slunk around in the shadows, waiting to ambush her as she sought to destroy them. At the request of Shetwea, she took on the role of Shuu's protector while he and Muut worked to defeat the giants, who created the Whispers.

The Whispers' name seemed misleading at first. The creatures screeched, an ear-piercing noise, whenever they were around. However, they moved silently right before they attacked, thus earning them their name. Their cries still haunted the goddess. Maah-res let out an involuntary growl as she remembered her deadly enemies.

Once she was satisfied with the sharpness of her claws, the panther inspected them before pacing her home.

"Muut must be out of her mind if she thinks she can ask me to go back," she grumbled.

The goddess walked over to a deer carcass and slashed through its body. Her claws went smoothly through the top layer of skin without snagging. Raising her paw to examine her nails, she nodded to herself.

"Maarduk thinks that just because he's her son, he can ask for anything."

The panther's ears flattened briefly before relaxing. She couldn't blame him for his impertinence, after all, he was just a cub. They were always too prideful and could not see that they were overstepping their bounds. If she'd had any, she would have given them a good smack with her heavy paw.

Taking a deep breath, Maah-res made her way over to her viewing pool. The pool lay in the center of her cave, its waters sparkling off the walls, creating delicate patterns. Dipping a single digit into the pool, she stirred it three times. The water rippled with the little whirlpool that she created. Once she pulled her paw out of the water, it became smooth and clear, like glass.

Staring deep into the water, the panther focused on where she wanted to go. Verdant fields were dotted with red clay homes. Looking around, she tried to find her pool's twin. She scanned through the Taal-baht mountains, weaving through the trees until she found a secluded spot deep in the woods.

Satisfied that there was no one around, Maah-res took a deep breath and stepped into the cool waters. N'aanzthal and

Shuu became a blur as she crossed through the dimensions. She hated traveling; it always made her dizzy. After what felt like a lengthy period of time, the distortion cleared. Before she knew it, her head broke through the pond. The goddess gasped for breath as she pulled herself out of the waters. Shaking herself off, she looked around before slinking off.

▼△▼

Maah-res twitched her whiskers and sniffed the warm air. She could smell her prey in the distance. A low growl escaped her lips as the great panther slowly made her way down the Taal-baht Mountains. Her giant padded feet masked any noise beneath her feet on the leaf-covered ground. Not even a twig snapped under the mighty beast.

The panther's eyes darted side-to-side, taking in the world she once knew. It'd been too long since she'd last walked through the mountains. Maah-res froze as she heard a leaf crunch nearby. Crouching down to hide, the great panther watched as a yak pass by, grazing on the long grasses nearby. Maah-res' tail twitched as she followed the beast. Her legs lightly shifted as she prepared to pounce. The yak raised its head and froze, listening. Its nose wiggled as it sniffed.

Her body tense, Maah-res fought the urge to snatch up the yak. She waited until the creature went back to grazing and slowly ambled off. Once the yak was gone, Maah-res straightened up and continued on her way down Taal-baht. Her ears twitched occasionally, keeping alert for any other creatures close by.

The shadows began to lengthen in the afternoon by the time that Maah-res exited the mountains. Homes of mud and red clay dotted the open field. Long grasses blew gently in the wind as the great panther stalked towards the village, crouching low so that she was partially concealed. A small group of children ran out from the homes and into the open area. Their screams echoing in the air.

Maah-res dropped to her belly, back legs wriggling as she prepared to ambush the group. Her claws protruded from her paws and kneaded the earth, turning up a rich brown soil. The panther's tail jerked side-to-side as her body tensed. One small child broke away from the party, chasing a rabbit that bounded out towards the mountains. With a snap, Maah-res pounced.

The great panther bounded towards the child, catching him by surprise. The boy froze as the feline raced towards him. After a couple seconds, he seemed to break from his shock and turned away screaming. The other children looked up and watched the beast quickly cover the ground between them. Panic erupted and they sped back to the safety of their homes. Men and women rushed out of the buildings, startled by the outburst, when they were greeted with children darting past them. One of the men looked up and noticed the panther chasing a young boy.

"Get everyone to the shrine!" the man called out.

The adults quickly grabbed the shrieking children and raced to the shrine. Taking a deep breath, the lone man ran the other way, towards the mighty god and lone child. Scooping up the boy, he turned sharply and ran back to what he hoped would be safety.

Maah-res let out a frustrated growl as her prey was getting away. Pushing herself harder, she worked to close the gap.

Pulling herself from her tunnel vision, she noticed that she didn't hear any screaming anymore. Glancing around, she saw empty fields. Facing forward once more, she watched as the man and child entered a shrine to Khons.

Letting out a mighty roar, Maah-res stopped short of the sanctuary and began pacing. Children whimpered as the women attempted to calm them. After circling the temple many times, the panther lay down in front of the temple entrance, staring inside at the terrified people. She couldn't enter Khons' holy home. She would wait, for now.

VII

THE EVENING AIR BLEW gently against Chione's face. After their meeting with Asim and his wife, Femi insisted that the two take a rare trip into Shuu for a quiet dinner away from the temple. As they walked through the streets eating honeycakes and sipping guava nectar, Chione found herself thinking of her family. Her parents used to take her and her brother out for guava and cakes every week, taking in the beauty of the setting sun together as they sat on nearby stones or soft grass.

A butterfly of excitement fluttered in her stomach as she smiled at these memories. Soon, once she'd finished her training and took over as the new shamasal of Shuu, she hoped to be able to walk with her family once more. There might even be a new baby for her to hug in her lap if Meskhet's union with Ashatiqa took place in the near future. Beside her, Femi hummed happily, small golden flowers popping up along their path in time with her song.

Chione found herself smiling back at those who dipped their heads to the shamasal in reverence. The discomfort she usually felt could not melt the serenity that she was feeling that night. After speaking with the high chief, Chione had told Femi in great detail about her vision. Her mentor praised her heavily, never taking away from Chione's success by bringing up whatever had upset her. Chione's usual curiosity disappeared as she allowed herself to enjoy her first positive experience with the gods.

A streak of pink smeared across the heavens as the two continued on. The soft buzzing of a bee floated by her ear, drawing an unconscious smile from Chione. The Subira's were happily at home, no doubt praising both her and the gods. They may even be leaving her a small offering outside their home to Chione for her part in saving their son. A warm flush crept across her face as she silently scolded herself for daring to believe that she would be worshipped like the gods.

"You've saved many lives today." Femi's voice suddenly breaking the tranquility of the evening startled Chione, pulling her from her thoughts.

"What?" she asked.

"You've saved many lives," Femi repeated. "If it weren't for you, sacrificing our people may still have continued. You should be proud. Your vision and actions are cause for celebration."

"Do you think they would do that?"

"I plan to talk to Honorable Mother tomorrow to see if we can arrange a little festival in your honor," Femi admitted, smiling as her words brought a flush to Chione's cheeks.

"I — th-thank you!" Chione stuttered. The butterfly that had been fluttering in her stomach moments before erupted into many that rapidly flew about, leaving her feeling giddy.

"Come," Femi said, "let's go home. We've earned ourselves a nice rest and peaceful morning tomorrow."

VIII

MAAH-RES CAUGHT THE SCENT of another village a-little-ways away. Her ears twitched as she listened to see if she could make out anything from the other village. She caught the voices of men talking together mixed with the grunting of yaks. Children could also be heard shouting and laughing. Maah-res' tail flopped side-to-side as she decided what to do. Would it be better to wait the group out, or sneak up on the other villagers?

Her whiskers shuddered, picking up on vibrations from the community next door. It didn't seem too far away. Glancing towards the temple's entrance, she sighed as she spied the residents still huddled deep in the heart of the shrine.

"Why did there have to be a home for Khons here?" Maah-res asked. Her words came out as a low growl that blended in with the chirping of the birds and rustling of the tall grasses. "If only it was one of the others'. They wouldn't have minded if I entered their place of reverence."

The sound of the villagers inside the sanctuary talking helped the mighty panther to make up her mind. With a silent jolt, Maah-res stood up and took off towards the neighboring village. As she pushed off from into a run, her claws digging deep gouges into the soft soil, tearing up the bright green grass and mixing it with the rich brown soil.

Wind blew in her face as the goddess raced towards the village. She quickly passed over a large swath of field before she was forced to slow down and stopped. The scent of a herd of yaks just a little way away. Despite the lack of coverage, Maah-res crouched down and resumed her advance at a slower pace.

The afternoon sun was still heavy in the sky before the village came into view. A large wooden paddock housed the long-haired yaks. The beasts grunted as they grazed in the enclosure. A solitary man walked out of the corral, a switch in his hand. The man locked the latch and made his way towards the village proper.

Maah-res' lips curled up in a snarl as she flattened herself against the ground. Her eyes scanned the perimeter of the community. It was much larger than the previous one. The wind had stopped blowing, leaving the tall grasses standing still. The yak enclosure was in prominent view of the rest of the town.

At the heart of the village, the panther spied a temple. Squinting at the stone structure, she tried to discern who's home the shrine belonged to. With a low growl, Maah-res worked to reposition herself a bit to see if she could find any distinguishing markings on the building. Scooting on her belly, the beast inched her way to the right. On the side of the shrine, a painting of Shetwea was visible. With a growl of frustration, Maah-res stopped crawling and laid down on her stomach once more.

"Shetwea, no good. Maarduk couldn't make this easy for me. Once I'm done here, he'll have to have a good reason to ask for my assistance again."

Scanning the village once more, Maah-res looked for any soul that would be close enough to reach before reaching the safety of the shrine.

No one.

"Maarduk be damned," Maah-res muttered, "I'm doing him a favor. If he wants me to prove his point, I'll do it my way."

Maah-res' sights settled on the red clay home closest to her. Her stomach rumbled and her eyes drifted to the conveniently corralled yaks. She licked her lips. It'd been too long since she'd truly tasted flesh. Making up her mind, Maah-res inched her way towards the enclosure, going the long way around to keep herself downwind.

As she approached the paddock, several of the yaks began grunting in earnest, unsure as to what was bothering them. The panther's lips curled over her teeth as she smiled at how easy this was turning out to be. She spied a singular yak standing away from the main group. The solitary beast stomped its feet and let out a distressed grunt. Several other yaks grunted in response. With a quick swipe of her massive paw, Maah-res broke one of the sides of the enclosure before snatching the lone yak and retreating into the grass.

Chaos erupted in the paddock as the remaining yaks grunted in panic and stumbled over each other in an attempt to escape the enclosure. One by one, as they freed themselves from their confinement, the distressed beasts ran into the heart of the village, flattening part of the garden in the process.

Maah-res watched in satisfaction as a few of the bovines knocked down one of the villagers and nearly trampled them to death.

Cries rang out as people rushed out to calm the terrified animals and tend to the wounded. More than one person was being helped up, eyes dazed and blood dripping from their head. A low chuckle escaped from the great panther as she finished up her meal.

It took a great effort for the residents to herd the frightened beasts back to the center of the town. Once the yaks were contained and began settling down, a couple men walked over to inspect the corral. Maah-res heard them marveling at how the paddock broke. Both mentioned the possibility of having to tie the beasts to poles in the town and going out early the next day to gather more wood to fix the side.

Maah-res lay silently, waiting for the men to get closer. It wouldn't do for her to waste too much energy considering what she was about to do. Better to just be patient.

Gradually, the villagers were able to tie up the yaks to a couple of posts in the center of the town. A teenaged boy was tasked with watching over them. Maah-res observed the delegation of yak duty as the remainder of the population resumed their daily tasks. The men who examined the broken pen earlier returned to the enclosure with a length of rope and some pieces of wood. They chatted amongst themselves as they made their way to the paddock. Upon reaching the pen, they set to work hammering the splintered beams together with the new slats of wood. To further enforce the repair, they wrapped the rope around the beams.

Maah-res tensed up as the men got closer and closer to her. Her claws protracted and retracted in quick succession, making furrows in the ground. Tail swishing, the panther waited for just the right moment.

One of the men turned to ask his partner a question, leaving his back exposed to the goddess. Before the other could respond, Maah-res struck. She leapt out of the tall grasses and snatched up the closest person in her mouth. The man cried out in surprise and pain as she crunched down on his torso. The other man snapped his head to look at his companion and let out a shout of dismay as he watched his friend die. Maah-res let out a satisfied snarl as bones crunched in her mouth.

The remaining man broke out of his paralysis, making a run for the village. His cries for help brought the shepherd out to look and others from their homes. The man waved his arms, calling out for his neighbors to get to safety. He neared the edge of the town, he stumbled, just barely.

"Run!" he called out, his breathless in his panic.

Eyes widened as the man entered the village. People called out to him, asking what was wrong. In a flash, Maah-res rounded the corner and picked up the running villager in her maw, shaking him like a ragdoll before biting down on him.

Screams of panic rang in the air as people raced towards the temple of Shetwea. Children cried as they were carried by anyone bigger than them to safety.

Maah-res took her time with her second victim as she enjoyed the chaos that she created. She let the remaining villagers reach the sanctuary, content in the death that she'd caused so far. The goddess tossed the body towards the herd of yaks, startling them. The yaks grunted in terror as they tried to hide from the great panther once more.

The goddess turned her attentions to the homes. She went to the nearest house and started kicking walls. After many kicks, she broke through the red clay. Roaring with delight, Maah-res methodically began destroying the village.

IX

A SHRINE MAIDEN MOVED through the temple, cleaning while the two shamasal trained. As Chione hummed her tune, the young girl began to feel a bit drowsy. Rubbing her eyes, she tried to wake herself up. Many a times she'd felt exhausted in the stuffy shrine, especially when the incense burned. When Chione changed her tone to the more guttural one, the maiden's eyes closed and she fell to the ground.

Femi and Chione sat on the floor of their shrine, meditating. Birds chirped in the warm afternoon sun as the two sat quietly. Chione hummed softly to herself, a high, light-hearted sound, as she concentrated. At her feet, a small, golden caterpillar crawled on the floor. Her tune became more guttural, causing the caterpillar to climb up a cattail that materialized with the change in the tone. The little caterpillar began releasing silken spindles around itself, creating a cocoon.

Femi's eyes slowly opened. Meditation always made her sleepy. It didn't help that Chione excelled in sedation techniques. The older woman listened to her student's technique.

Chione changed her tone once more and her pitch became much higher. The notes took on a frantic quality, causing Femi to become more alert and waking up the slumbering maiden. The young girl looked around, her face red as she spied the mistress of the temple watching her get off of the floor.

The cocoon began to tremble as the caterpillar tried to break free. Chione's frantic notes matching the shaking of the cocoon. Suddenly, the young shaman stopped humming and became quiet. Femi watched her ward with an attentive eye. The girl's brow furrowed and sweat beaded on her brow. Femi placed her hand on Chione's head and began singing softly. Her notes were sweet and calmed the young shaman. Keeping her hand on her ward's head, Femi started chanting in a deep, commanding tone.

Images from Chione's mind played out in hers. Femi watched as a group of villagers from one of the outer villages huddled close together in the shrine of Khons. Children wept quietly as their mothers tried to soothe them. Tentatively, one of the men in the temple inched towards the entrance. He got within a couple feet before freezing up and turning back around in defeat.

Femi's chant became more earnest, drawing on the visions that her ward was seeing. Another village on the outskirts of Shuu. Inside the temple of Shetwea, the populace stood crammed within his walls. Their faces were pale, eyes red and puffy, as they watched the form of a large feline move around outside. Low growls and snarls could be heard, in addition to the grunting of yaks and the occasional sound of something falling down.

With great focus, Femi's chanting slowed down and she opened her eyes. She stood inside the temple, surrounded by the huddled masses. Everyone ignored her as she walked to the entrance of the shrine. Squinting her eyes, Femi brought one hand up to shield her face from the sun. She was greeted with several homes in ruin. Turning her head side-to-side, Femi tried to see the great beast. A crash behind her caused her to slowly circle the outside of the Shetwea's sanctuary. Femi watched as a giant panther pulled its foot out of a clay wall.

"Maah-res..." she whispered.

The cat looked up from what she was doing and locked eyes with Femi. Her black slits constricting in her yellow eyes. With a mighty roar, the panther turned and took off running.

Femi's eyes popped open as she gasped for breath. She grabbed Chione by the shoulder and roughly shook her.

"Wake up, child!"

Chione's eyes snapped open. "What's going on?"

"Didn't you see?" Femi asked.

Chione shook her head. "I started to see something, but I figured it was the incense drawing me into a dream."

"We must warn the people. Maah-res has woken up and is headed towards us."

The clatter of a bronze bowl on the floor distracted the two. The temple maiden stared at the dropped bowl in horror and stammered an apology. "I'm sorry, Mistress. Did you say that the great panther is coming?"

"Go to Holy Father and tell him to get everyone into Baah-re as soon as possible," Femi commanded. The girl hesitated in her fear. "Go!" Femi ordered.

Spinning around, the girl bolted out of the shrine and down the worn stone street.

"Femi," Chione said softly, "what are we going to do? We can't possibly stop a god."

"Come, child, we must keep the mighty panther from entering the heart of Shuu."

As she looked at the fear in Chione's face even as the young girl nodded in agreement, Femi felt her stomach drop as she turned to leave the temple. She could see no way to stop the rampaging goddess.

▼△▼

Chione's breath caught in her throat as she ran behind her master. She was surprised at how fit her master was, especially considering Femi was telling everyone to go to the god's temple. Though they moved quickly, Femi did not appear to be short of breath.

"Femi!" Chione called out. "Is this because of my vision with the gods?" The idea had come to her earlier, but as they continued heading east, Chione couldn't shake the feeling that this was somehow her fault.

Femi did not respond at first. She dodged around a group of women walking in the street, barking at them to get to safety before turning down a side-street. As they neared the edge of the main city of Shuu, Femi finally spoke.

"I don't think so. Blessed Khons came to you, Chione. He would not lead you astray." Femi slowed down to a brisk walk so that she could answer properly.

"Then why is the great panther punishing us?"

"Some of the pantheon are not as merciful as Blessed Khons or Muut. Maah-res is usually like Shetwea, aloof from the main gods. However, if she feels as though the gods have been slighted, she may have been convinced to act on behalf of another."

Chione shook her head, distressed at the news. If Khons and Muut supported the change, why would the other gods go against that and punish her people?

The questions hadn't slowed Femi down much. The pair sped through the streets, nearing the fields on the outskirts of the main city. Chione was breathing heavily, but she managed to ask, "Are we going to be able to stop her?"

Femi shrugged. "I don't know," she replied. "This is un-precedented. I can't think of any time in recent history where the gods have walked among us. The texts mention it during the Dark Times, but nothing else."

Chione continued on in silence, trying to recall anything she could from school and her training regarding the Dark Times. All she could think of were the murals depicting great Maah-res chasing down their ancestors amidst the burning capital.

She walked into Femi's outstretched arm and stopped, rubbing her chest. Her master stood, tense, staring off into the distance. Chione began to ask why they stopped when Femi motioned for her to be quiet. Several moments went by before Femi spoke.

"Chione —" Femi began.

A mighty roar rent the air, and Chione found herself trembling as tears welled at the corners of her eyes. Her breath caught in her chest as an angry Maah-res stood at the opposite end of the meadow, tail swinging back and forth and ears back. The panther growled, baring her teeth.

"Chione, we must act fast," Femi said softly. "If we strike first, we may catch her off-guard and gain an advantage."

Chione let out a squeak in response. Her eyes were locked onto the mighty panther's, her legs feeling weak. Her mind had gone blank the instant she saw the great panther goddess. How was she supposed to take on an angry god? Why had she tried to change things in the first place?

"Chione," Femi whispered.

Maah-res began crossing the length of the pitch, slowly picking up speed with each step.

"Chione," Femi said a little louder. "Chione!"

Chione stood silently, frozen in place. She tried several times to speak but found that her voice would not work. Her mouth worked to form a response, trying to say anything, even something to encourage herself. Not even her eyes could focus; she didn't see anything other than the beast charging at her.

The panther goddess was now jogging towards the two, covering the distance between them in long strides. Her teeth were barred and claws extended as she neared the two quickly.

"Chione!" Femi called out, shaking her shoulders.

Chione blinked slowly, eyes finally focusing on the woman in front of her. Her legs gave way, but Femi caught her. Singing out a commanding note, Chione felt a measure of warmth and strength flow through her.

"Chione," Femi said sternly. "Focus. We can do this. Khons and Mother Muut are on our side."

Chione nodded. Taking a deep breath, she raised her hands and steeled herself. *Femi is right,* Chione thought. Khons and Mother Muut were on their side. This is what she'd been training for, and she wasn't going to let an angry god destroy her home.

"Ready, Chione?" Femi asked, turning to face the quickly approaching feline.

Chione sucked in one more breath. "I'm ready."

Standing side-by-side, the two women began to sing.

It was a simple song, Femi singing the lower alto notes while Chione sang a higher soprano note. Their voices wove together in harmony, echoing in the open field. Maah-res let out an earth-shaking roar and lunged at the two women. With a jar, the panther stopped just short of the pair.

Both Chione and Femi faced the goddess with their hands outstretched. Golden threads wrapped around the panther's back legs, preventing her from reaching the shamasal. As thick as ivy, the threads wove into the ground like tree roots, pulling the panther's hindlegs down with them.

Maah-res struggled to free herself, but the steady harmonies coming from the shamasal prevented her from doing so. Chione stood with her eyes closed, singing with a purity that strengthened her hold on the panther. Maah-res snarled.

I have to stay strong, she thought.

Chione's eyes snapped open, and she glanced at her mentor as she continued the song. Femi, maintaining eye contact with Maah-res, began circling around the great panther, her hands motioning a weaving movement. Her voice dropped into her lower register, alternating between ululation and grunts as she laced together a rope of golden threads. With each movement of her hand, a stronger bond knotted together around the goddess' torso, pulling her back further away from Chione. Sweat beaded on Femi's brow as she tried to force the feline into a sitting position.

Chione changed her song and began singing softly, coaxing the mighty Maah-res into a deep sleep. Her hands moved in slow, mesmerizing circles. She stared deeply into the goddess' eyes, trying to transfer her will onto the great beast.

Maah-res snarled, her head shaking. It was almost as if she were crying, "You will not dominate me!" But the only thing Chione heard was a menacing growl.

In a sing-song voice, Chione pleaded, "Please, Blessed Maah-res. All we want is to live in peace. We meant no disrespect. Blessed Khons and Holy Muut gave us their blessing to save the boy."

Her entreaty had a pleasant inflection that caused Maah-res' eyes to droop slightly. With another growl, the goddess seemed to snap herself out of the trance. She pushed with her legs, gaining a little traction and almost muscling herself out of the sitting position. Femi gave a bark and pulled back with her hands on an invisible rope so hard that she stumbled and fell.

Chione's gaze flicked over to her mento, who was still sitting on the ground. Femi redoubled her efforts, working to create another layer of rope to secure the panther's hindlegs. Weaving her hands together once more, she began her ululations and grunting as she bound the feline to the earth. Golden threads knitted together, forming the rope, but Chione noticed the strands becoming thinner.

Come on, Femi, she thought as she continued her soothing circles and gentle lilt. *Just a little more.*

Chione gazed as Maah-res, who had stopped struggling. Chione took a tentative step forward, never stopping her song. With a lurch, Maah-res tried to break free of her bonds, swiping at Chione. She jumped back in shock but managed to keep her voice steady. The ivy-like bindings on her legs and Femi's torso ropes held, keeping Chione safe.

This isn't enough, Chione thought. So, Chione dug deep within and changed the tone of her voice. Instead of her gentle singing, suggesting that sleep would be pleasant, her tone became more commanding, telling the goddess that she *will* be sleeping. Her hands still moved in mesmerizing circles, calming the big cat down.

Maah-res' eyes began to droop once more. After several tense minutes, a weak growl escaped her. Her eyes closed briefly. Maah-res struggled to open her eyes once more, working to shake the soothing power of Chione's magic.

Finally, it looked like Maah-res was no longer taut. Chione wanted to ask Femi if they were done, if it was enough, but she kept singing. Instead, her gaze flickered to her mentor, who was staring at the panther's legs. Femi changed her wordless song to a prayer to Khons in the ancient language.

"Almighty Khons, watch over your children.

The danger is close, but through you we are strong.

Wrap us in your arms.

Through you, we are protected."

Maah-res' ears twitched.

Femi gasped.

Chione took a step closer to the goddess. With a noticeable movement, Maah-res' shoulders slumped as her front legs dropped to their knees. Femi began singing with renewed vigor. Her voice rang out in the early evening air.

Chione returned to her soothing song and slowly made her way to the goddess. Her hand movements got smaller and smaller as she neared the drooping panther. Maah-res' eyes were half open and the snarl was all but gone from her lips. Chione's eyes softened as she got close enough to touch the great panther. She reached out and tentatively placed her hand on Maah-res's nose. The goddess looked up at the girl with drowsy eyes. There was a disappointment in her eyes. Chione stared deep within the yellow eyes and tried touch the goddess' mind.

"Sleep," Chione whispered.

With a massive yawn, Maah-res closed her eyes and laid down. Her body rose and fell in the gentle rhythm of one who was deep asleep. She purred softly, convincing Chione that the goddess was not pretending to be asleep.

We did it, Chione thought. *Almost.*

Working quickly, she sang a low song to coax the tall grasses to cover the slumbering panther. Strands of grass knitted together, creating a small mound in the middle of the field. As the blades thickened and strengthened, the golden threads that bound Maah-res to the earth disappeared.

With a sigh, Chione dropped to her knees. Femi walked over to her and placed her hand on Chione's shoulder.

"Well done, my child," she said with a smile.

Panting slightly from her exertions, Chione returned the smile. "Thank you. I couldn't have done it without you."

X

EVERAL DAYS HAD PASSED since Chione and Femi bound
Maah-res in the tall grasses. The two had spent most of the
time meditating, since using that much energy drained them
on many levels. Not only were they physically fatigued, but
their mental and spiritual psyches were exhausted and needed
rest. During that time, a number of people got together and began repairing the damage to the homes in the outer city that
were ruined by the goddess.

Now, a large crowd gathered before Chione as she stood on
the dais next to High Chief Asim and his wife. To her surprise,
Chione found that she would rather face the snarling panther
goddess again instead of facing all of Shuu. Swallowing a large
lump in her throat, Chione worked to keep her body from trembling.

The audience quieted as Asim raised his hands.

"My children, today we celebrate the defeat of Maah-res.
With the assistance of her god-given powers, Sister Chione has
provided Shuu with her protection."

The people cheered and chanted praises to both the gods and Chione, causing the young woman to blush. Scanning the crowd, Chione looked for her mentor. However, she was unable to find Femi anywhere.

Asim began speaking once again, but Chione didn't focus on his words. She was too busy looking for Femi.

"Why isn't Femi up here with me?" Chione had asked her chief before the ceremony.

"Sister Femi said it was you who subdued Maah-res. She wanted you to get all of the recognition," Asim replied.

"It is such an honor to be given such responsibility by the shaman," Eshe added. "Sister Femi has always thought highly of you. It's no surprise that she would want you to be given all the credit that you deserve." Eshe beamed at the young shaman.

"I suppose," Chione said. "It just doesn't feel right."

More cheering erupted from the crowd once Asim finished his speech. Chione glanced at the high chief who nodded at her. Waving her hand sheepishly, Chione tried to smile at her people, as though she believed that she was worthy of their adoration. Inside, all she felt was a sham. That she should at least be sharing this ceremony. It was Femi, after all, who had snapped Chione out of her state of shock. Chione surely would've perished if it weren't for Femi.

Finally, the noise of the crowd died down as Asim motioned for them to disperse. The warriors jogged off towards the tchlatsi pitch in preparation for the special game in Chione's honor. All of Shuu's best athletes would be participating in this event, unlike during Tepet when only some of them would be.

Rumors were that even Po'tchai would be coming out of tchlatsi retirement and playing.

Chione made her way off the dais, her mind numb. Her inability to find Femi made her uncomfortable. Hordes of people stopped in front of her and offered their respects, touching their foreheads to her hand and giving a small blessing. Their faces blurred together until Chione lost track of how many people came to her. Dozens? A hundred? She couldn't remember. All she wanted to do was find her mentor.

Her family came running up to her, closely followed by Yahya's. Chione smiled briefly as she saw young Tarik standing next to his mother.

"Sister Chione," Nena said. "We owe you so much. First you save our little Nkosi, and then you face down one of the gods because of us. What can we do to repay you?"

Nena dropped to her knees and held Chione's hand against her forehead. Yahya and the rest of her family followed suit, bowing their heads in respect to the young shaman.

"I — I did what I thought was right," Chione said lamely, her cheeks burning. "We should no longer have to sacrifice our people to the gods just to make sure that nothing bad happens if we don't get a new shaman. I don't want anything."

Not lifting her head from Chione's hand, Nena pressed, "Sister, we owe you a great debt. You don't have to name your desire now. When the time is right, you will know what you want."

Before Chione could protest, Nena stood up and kissed Chione both on the hand and the cheeks. Her family got up with her. Edu bent down and kissed Chione on the forehead in a fatherly fashion.

"Come," Edu said to his family, "let us leave Sister Chione to speak with her family."

Yahya, Tarik and their sister waved at Chione and moved off towards the tchlatsi field. Edu and Nena followed behind.

Chione turned to face her family as they stood off to the side. Her father beamed at her, as did her mother, albeit with tears rimming her eyes. Meskhet stood with his arm around Ashatiqa while Nkosi watched his big sister in awe.

"Oh, my little Chione," Naeemah gushed. "I'm so proud of you. You've become such a blessing to our family." Naeemah walked over and pulled her daughter in a tight embrace.

Chione felt her eyes get hot as her head rested against her mother's bosom. She felt like a little girl again, craving her mother's comfort after a bad dream. How could such a simple action cause her to unravel so much? Giving in to the myriad of emotions swirling within her, Chione found herself crying in her mother's arms.

"I've caused so many problems," she choked out. "How could anyone think of honoring me? Femi should be getting all of the praise."

Khafra walked over and rubbed his daughter's back. "Chione, you deserve everything you've received."

"You've *talked* to the gods," Naeemah said emphatically. "Not only did they choose you worthy enough to speak to them, but they listened to your suggestion and allowed for us to go from human sacrifices to animal. Do you know how few people have actually managed that?"

"But people have died because I angered the gods. Maahres wouldn't have been sent to punish us if I made the right decision."

"When have the gods ever agreed on anything?" Khafra asked. "They're constantly arguing amongst themselves. They would've found a reason to 'punish' us eventually."

Chione lifted her head from her mother's chest and wiped away her tears. She hiccupped a couple of times before pulling away from her mother's embrace. Chione straightened her dress and hair in an attempt to regain her composure. Taking a few steadying breaths, she nodded.

"You're right," Chione finally said. "It's just difficult to accept. The praise should go to Femi, but I couldn't even find her at the celebration. I don't know why she would leave me like this."

Running her hands through her daughter's hair, Naeemah made a soft, soothing sound. "Femi would never leave you. You probably just overlooked her. Honorable Father did make sure that all of Shuu was in attendance. I even heard that some people from Qateh came over to see the girl who subdued a god. You're famous."

"I don't want to be famous," Chione pouted.

No sooner did the words leave her mouth did she drop her eyes in embarrassment. It wasn't her parents' fault that she was the recipient of great praise. She was too old to be acting like a child throwing a tantrum.

"I'm sorry," Chione said softly. "I just want to speak with Femi."

"NaeNae," Meskhet spoke up. "I saw her earlier today, standing in the field. You may want to try there."

"Thank you, Meskhet," Chione said. "I'll go check there."

Khafra motioned to his boys to start moving. Speaking to his daughter, he asked, "Will you be going to the tchlatsi game? We would love it if you sat with us."

"I plan on it. I will if I can speak to Femi first," she replied.

Chione went to each family member and gave them a big hug. When she got to her parents, she held on for a few seconds longer, squeezing her eyes closed to fight back tears once more.

"Stay strong, little one," Naeemah whispered to her daughter. "The gods chose you for a reason. Don't doubt yourself."

Breaking out of her mother's embrace, Chione nodded her head and wiped her eye.

Chione watched as her family walked away, heading out to catch up with the rest of Shuu to watch the big game. Her spirit felt drained, as though she had used her skills for an extended period of time once more. As soon as they were out of her sight, the young woman let out a massive sigh and turned to find her master.

Winding through the empty city streets, Chione kept her eyes peeled for Femi. Seeing the roads and buildings abandoned made her feel discomfited. There should have been at least a few stragglers making their way over to the tchlatsi field. However, there was no one. The silence was intense. Chione picked at her fingers a bit as she walked, something she'd never done before. Looking around, she nearly tripped. Doing a quick stutter-step to maintain her balance, she tried to find what caused her to lose her balance. Behind her, she saw the back end of a mau darting away. Before the cat went around the corner of a house, it gave her a withering glare, annoyed that she woke him up from his nap.

Chione chuckled to herself, trying to lighten the tension she felt within. "Well, I wanted to run into one soul right now. I guess a mau is acceptable."

She continued on until she reached the edge of the main part of the city. Ahead of her lay the open field surrounded by trees, the Taal-baht mountains rising in the distance. There was a hill in the center of the field, and a person was standing next to it. Chione picked up her pace, hoping that Meskhet was right and Femi was now only a short way away.

With her hair tied in her characteristic braids and wrapped around her head, Femi walked around the hill, her focus deep within as she moved slowly along the perimeter. Chione caught up to her and tapped her gently on the shoulder.

"Hello, my child," Femi said, a hint of sadness tinging her voice. "Why are you not at the ceremony?"

"Why weren't you there? You deserve as much praise as I do," Chione said breathlessly. She worked to keep down the flood of emotions that lay just beneath the surface, threatening to bubble over and consume her.

Femi continued to observe the hill silently. She walked with her hands behind her back. Chione followed her, waiting for an answer. When Femi didn't respond, Chione gave a small sigh.

"Shuu no longer needs me," Femi finally said.

Her shoulders were no longer strong and proud as she walked. The older woman's face did not contain its customary glow. She appeared haggard and her eyes were puffy, as though she had not been sleeping well.

"What are you talking about? Of course, Shuu needs you."

Femi ignored her question. Marveling at Chione's handiwork from a few days ago, she said, "Isn't it amazing how the blades of grass bent to your will, providing such a strong covering for Maah-res? They cover her completely." Femi gestured to the barely visible panther buried within. "I heard that Honorable Father wants to call this Maah-nhen, 'we are judged'. A fitting name, don't you think?"

Femi turned to Chione to see her reaction.

"I suppose that is a good name," Chione said. "But Femi, why are you acting like this? Come back with me, you deserve to be honored. Without you, we all would've perished. I only did this with your help and guidance."

Femi's eyes were sad as she watched her protégé. "Chione, I lost my gift while we were engaged with Maah-res. You are now the new shaman. My job is done."

Chione stared at her mentor in shock. "What are you talking about? We bound Maah-res to the earth together." She didn't understand what Femi was talking about. Chione remembered the confrontation with Maah-res and how Femi's singing also worked to bind the goddess. How could she have done that if her gift was lost?

Femi shook her head. "No, my child. My power disappeared shortly after I bound her torso. You did all that on your own."

Unable to believe what she was hearing, Chione ignored the million questions that came to her mind and focused on one thing. Femi's attitude was starting to scare her, and she didn't want to lose to the fear. "Come back with me, Femi," she begged. "Let's go watch tchlatsi together. We never got to see the game during Tepet."

"I have been a shaman since I was seventeen, Chione. I am almost fifty. This is all I've known. Now that I am no longer a shaman, what do I have to go back to?" The woman's hands shook slightly as she spoke. "My family is dead. I have no children. You were all I had. Now I don't even have you."

Tears ran down Femi's cheeks as she spoke. They also ran down Chione's.

"You will always be part of my family," Chione said as she wiped her eyes. "You are like an auntie to me. I'm sure my family will welcome you with open arms. Besides, Shuu owes you a great debt for all that you've done for them. Surely, they wouldn't dishonor and ignore you."

Femi ran her hands through the young woman's hair. "Oh, my darling girl. You are too young to remember the last shaman, my predecessor. She was in her thirties when I completed my training. Once Parvenah lost her powers, everyone's attentions shifted to me. When would I master my skills? When would I be able to help them with their problems? Would I be able to protect them from the gods? Parvenah no longer mattered. She melted into the background. Luckily for her, she wasn't too old to start a family, so she wasn't alone."

Chione opened and closed her mouth. She couldn't even begin to imagine the pain that her master was feeling.

"This isn't your problem though," Femi said. "You need to start mastering all of your techniques, making sure you can perform them on yourself and others. One thing I will say, don't let your position keep you above the people. You are the same as them. Don't let that stop you from having a family. They will be there for you when Shuu has forgotten."

The two women stood in silence in the shadow of Maah-nhen. Chione grabbed the older woman's hand. Femi smiled and gave it a squeeze. Wiping her eyes, Femi took a deep breath.

"Come, Chione. Let's go watch that game I promised you."

The sun hung low in the sky as the two neared the first streets. Wind blew across the field, causing the grass to bend. A ray of sunlight landed on Maah-nhen. Birds stopped chirping. A low growl could be heard from the hill. Slowly, all traces of Maah-res disappeared, replaced with dirt and stone. The bud of a singular golden flower sprouted out of the grass at the top of the hill, ready to bloom.

"What's happening?" Chione asked.

"Maah-res has returned to N'aanzthal," Femi replied. "Come, we'll miss Po'tchai if we hang around much longer."

Chione smiled at her mentor and the two began their return to the village. Behind them, the golden flower slowly opened, its petals sparkling in the light of the sun.

△▼△

About the Author

K.N. Nguyen is a fantasy author and founder of DragonScript. Growing up, she often found herself immersed in some imaginary world, conquering enemy nations, and saving the day. As time went on, her love for horrible puns and nerd culture pulled her out of these worlds and brought her back to reality.

It wasn't until she started working at her office job that she felt the itch to begin writing. Since 2015, she's been bringing her stories to life, one-by-one, and following her passion by delving into new mythologies.

A native of Sacramento, California, K.N. Nguyen spends her time singing karaoke, playing taiko, enjoying rhythm dancing games, and travelling with her friends and family when she isn't writing.

Other Works by K.N. Nguyen

The Fallen Series

King's Blood

Oath Blood

God's Blood

Nightmare Blood

Other Books

Dragon Script

Anthologies K.N. Nguyen Has Appeared In:

New Beginnings by DragonScript

New Adventures by DragonScript

Coffins & Dragons by Dragon Soul Press

The Once and Future Kingdom by Irish Horse Productions

Towards the Sun by DragonScript

First Stain by Inked in Grey

Another World by SummerStorm Press

Wicked West by SummerStorm Press

9 781949 322149